*"It's my nature no___
Killian warned.*

"It does take courage to talk," Susannah agreed, gathering her own. It would take courage to get to the root of his problem with her. "It's easier to button up and retreat into silence," she challenged more firmly.

"Let's drop this conversation."

Susannah stood in the doorway, feeling the tension radiating from around him. Her mouth grew dry. "No."

The one word, softly spoken, struck him solidly. "I learned a long time ago to say nothing. I'm a man with a lot of ugly secrets, Susannah. Secrets I'm not proud of. They're best left unsaid."

"I don't agree," she replied gently.

Killian lifted his chin and stared deeply into her luminous gray eyes. The need to confide, to open his arms and sweep her against him, was painfully real. But Killian didn't dare tell her the raw, blatant truth—that he wanted her in every way imaginable.

Dear Reader,

Welcome to Silhouette **Special Edition** . . . welcome to romance.

Last year, I requested your opinions on the books that we publish. Thank you for the many thoughtful comments. For the next couple of months, I'd like to share quotes with you from those letters. This seems very appropriate while we are in the midst of the THAT SPECIAL WOMAN! promotion. Each one of our readers is a *special* woman, as heroic as the heroines in our books.

Our THAT SPECIAL WOMAN! title for this month is *Kate's Vow,* by Sherryl Woods. You may remember Kate from Sherryl's VOWS trilogy. Kate has taken on a new client—and the verdict is love!

July is full of heat with *The Rogue* by Lindsay McKenna. This book continues her new series, MORGAN'S MERCENARIES. Also in store is Laurie Paige's *Home for a Wild Heart*—the first book of her WILD RIVER TRILOGY. And wrapping up this month of fireworks are books from other favorite authors: Christine Flynn, Celeste Hamilton and Bay Matthews!

I hope you enjoy this book, and all of the stories to come!

Sincerely,

Tara Gavin
Senior Editor

Quote of the Month: "I enjoy a well-thought-out romance. I enjoy complex issues—dealing with several perceptions of one situation. When I was young, romances taught me how to ask to be treated—what type of goals I could set my sights on. They really were my model for healthy relationships. The concept of not being able to judge 'Mr. Right' by first impressions helped me to find my husband, and the image of a strong woman helped me to stay strong."   —L. Montgomery, Connecticut

LINDSAY McKENNA

THE ROGUE

Silhouette®

SPECIAL EDITION®

Published by Silhouette Books New York

America's Publisher of Contemporary Romance

To my husband, David,
who has stuck with me through thick and thin,
making each year better than the last.

SILHOUETTE BOOKS
300 East 42nd St., New York, N.Y. 10017

THE ROGUE

Books by Lindsay McKenna

LINDSAY McKENNA

After the publication of *Return of a Hero* (SE #541), I received hundreds of letters asking what happened to the story's hero, Morgan Trayhern. Well, in my latest trilogy, *Morgan's Mercenaries*, the question is answered.

I loved returning to the characters of Morgan and his wife, Laura, and am thrilled to give you three very exciting, adventurous and intensely romantic stories about the men in Morgan Trayhern's employ.

Mercenaries have always fascinated me—they are loners in our world, with mysterious pasts and brooding secrets deep within their hearts. I hope you enjoy reading about Wolf, Killian and Jake as much as I did writing about them!

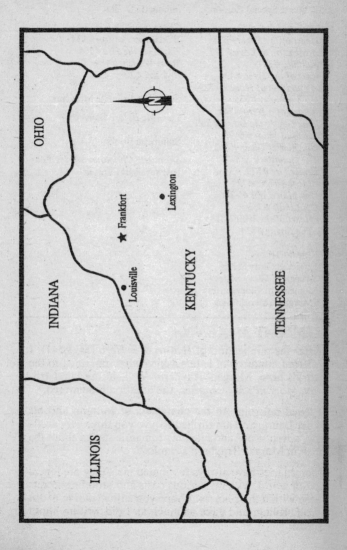

Prologue

"Killian, your next assignment is a personal favor to me."

Morgan Trayhern was sitting with his friend and employee in a small Philipsburg, Montana, restaurant. The situation with Wolf Harding and Sarah Thatcher had been successfully wrapped up, and now it was time to pack up and go home. Morgan grimaced apologetically, as Killian's features remained completely closed, only a glitter in his hard, intelligent blue eyes suggesting possible interest.

Morgan picked up a fork and absently rotated it between his fingers and thumb. They'd already ordered their meals, so now was as good a time as any to broach the topic. "Look," he began with an effort, purposely keeping his voice low, "whether I want to or not, I'm going to have to put you on an assignment involving a woman, Killian.''

Killian sat relaxed, his long, spare hands draped casually on his thighs as he leaned back in the poorly padded metal chair. But anyone who knew him knew he was never truly relaxed; he only gave that appearance. He stared guardedly at Morgan. "I can't."

Morgan stared back, the silence tightening between them. "You're going to have to."

Killian eased the chair down and placed his hands on the table. "I told you—I don't deal with women," he said flatly.

"At least hear me out," Morgan pleaded.

"It won't do any good."

Exhaustion shadowed Morgan's gray eyes. "Just sit there and listen."

Killian wrestled with an unexpected surge of panic that left a bitter taste in his mouth. He held Morgan's gaze warningly, feeling suddenly as if this man who had been his friend since their days in the French Foreign Legion had become an adversary.

Morgan rubbed his face tiredly. "The assignment deals with Laura's cousin from her mother's side of the family," he began, referring to his wife, who'd managed to befriend Killian—at least as much as Morgan had ever seen him allow. "This is important to me—and to Laura—and we want to know that you're the one handling the situation. It's personal, Killian."

Killian's scowl deepened, and his mouth thinned.

"Laura's cousin, Susannah Anderson, came to visit us in D.C." Morgan's eyes grew dark and bleak. "From what we've been able to piece together, on the way home, Susannah was at the bus station in Lexington, Kentucky, when a man came up and started a conversation with her. Moments later, he was shot right in front of her eyes. We think Susannah saw the murderer, Killian—and he shot her, too, because she was a witness. The bullet hit her skull, cracked it and exited. By some miracle, she doesn't have brain damage, thank God. But the injury's swelling left her in a coma for two months. She regained consciousness a month ago, and I was hoping she could give us a lead on her attacker, but she can't remember what he looked like. And another thing, Killian—she can't talk.''

Morgan rubbed his hands together wearily, his voice heavy with worry. ''The psychiatrists are telling me that the horror of the experience is behind her inability to speak, not brain damage. She's suppressed the whole incident—that's why she can't describe the killer. Laura went down and stayed with Susannah and her family in Kentucky for a week after Susannah was brought home from the hospital, in hopes that she'd find her voice again.'' Morgan shrugged. ''It's been a month now, and she's still mute.''

Killian shifted slightly, resting his hands on the knees of his faded jeans. ''I've seen that mute condition,'' he said quietly, ''in some of the children and women of Northern Ireland.''

Morgan opened his hands in a silent plea to Killian to take the assignment. ''That's not the whole story, Killian. I need you to guard Susannah. There's evidence to indicate that the killer will go after Susannah once he finds out she survived. I think Susannah was an innocent bystander in a drug deal gone bad, but so far we don't know enough to point any fingers. Susannah's memory is the key, and they can't risk her remembering the incident.

"Susannah was under local police guard at the Lexington hospital while she was there, and I had one of my female employees there, too. Since her release, I've told Susannah to stay on her parents' fruit farm in the Kentucky hills. Normally she lives and works down in the small nearby town of Glen, where she teaches handicapped children."

Morgan grasped the edge of the table, and his knuckles were white as he made his final plea. "She's family, Killian. Laura is very upset about this, because she and Susannah are like sisters. I want to entrust this mission to my very best man, and that's you."

Glancing sharply at his boss, Killian asked, "I'd be a bodyguard?"

"Yes. But Susannah and her parents aren't aware of the possible continued threat to her, so I don't want them to know your true capacity there. They're upset enough after nearly losing their daughter. I don't want to stress them more. Relaxation and peace are crucial to Susannah's recovery. I've contacted her father, Sam Anderson, and told him you're a friend of mine who needs some convalescence. Sam knows the type of company I run, and has an inkling of some of the things we do. I told him you were exhausted after coming in off a long-term mission and needed to hole up and rest."

Killian shrugged. The story wasn't too far from the truth. He hardened his heart. "I never take assignments involving women, Morgan."

"I know that. But I need you for this, Killian. On the surface, this assignment may look easy and quiet, but it's not. Stay on guard. I'm trying to track the drug deal right now. All our contacts in South America are checking it out, and I'm working closely with the Lexington police department. There's a possibility it could involve Santiago's cartel."

Killian's jaw clenched at the name of José Santiago, the violent Peruvian drug kingpin they'd finally managed to extradite and get behind bars.

Morgan gave Killian a pleading look. "Susannah's already been hurt enough in this ordeal. I don't want her hurt further. I worry that her family could become a target, too."

Cold anger wound through Killian as he thought about the mission. "Picking on a defenseless woman tells you the kind of slime we're dealing with."

Morgan gave Killian a probing look. "So will you take this assignment?"

Morgan knew that Killian's weakness, his Achilles' heel, was the underdog in any situation.

"One more thing," Morgan warned as he saw Killian's eyes thaw slightly. "Susannah isn't very emotionally stable right now. Her parents are Kentucky hill people. They're simple, hardworking folks. Sam owns a two-hundred-acre fruit farm, and that's their livelihood. Susannah ought to be in therapy to help her cope with what happened to her. I've offered to pay for it, but she's refusing all help."

"Frightened of her own shadow?" Killian asked, the face of his sister, Meg, floating into his memory.

Morgan nodded. "I want you to take care of Susannah. I know it's against your guidelines for a job, but my instincts say you're the right person to handle this situation—and her.''

His own haunted past resurfacing, tugging at his emotions, Killian felt his heart bleed silently for this woman and her trauma. Avoiding Morgan's searching gaze, he sat silently for a long time, mulling over his options. Finally he heaved a sigh and muttered, ''I just can't do it.''

''Dammit!'' Morgan leaned forward, fighting to keep his voice under tight control. ''I *need* you, Killian. I'm not *asking* you to take this assignment, I'm *ordering* you to take it.''

Anger leaped into Killian's narrowed eyes, and his fist clenched on the table's Formica top as he stared at Morgan. ''And if I don't take this assignment?''

''Then, whether I like it or not, I'll release you from any obligation to Perseus. I'm sorry, Killian. I didn't want the mission to come down to this. You're the best at what we do. But Susannah is part of my family.'' His voice grew emotional with pleading. ''Whatever your problem with women is, put it aside. I'm begging you to help Susannah.''

Killian glared at Morgan, tension radiating from him, every joint in his usually relaxed body stiff with denial. He *couldn't* protect a woman! Yet, as he stared at Morgan, he knew that if he didn't take the assignment his boss would release him from his duties with Perseus, and the money he made was enough to keep Meg reasonably well-off. If he hadn't come to work for Perseus, he'd never have been able to free her from the financial obligations brought on by her tragedy.

His need to help his sister outweighed the risk of his own pain. The words came out harshly, bitten off: "I'll do the best I can."

Relief showed on Morgan's taut features. "Good. My conscience is eating me alive on this situation, Killian. But this is the only way I can make amends to Susannah for what's happened. She was innocent—in the wrong place at the wrong time."

"I'll leave right away," Killian rasped as he took the voucher and airline ticket Morgan proffered. No use putting off the inevitable. He'd pick up his luggage at the motel across from the restaurant and get under way. No longer hungry, he rose from the booth. Morgan appeared grateful, but that didn't do anything for him. Still angry over Morgan's threat to fire him, Killian made his way outside without a word. Walking quickly, he crossed the street to the motel, his senses as always hyperalert to everything around him.

What kind of person was this Susannah Anderson? Killian wondered. He'd noticed Morgan's voice lower with feeling when he'd spoken about her. Was she young? Old? Married? Apparently not, if she was staying with her parents. A large part of him, the part that suffered and grieved over Meg, still warned him not to go to Kentucky. His soft spot for a woman in trouble was the one chink in his carefully tended armor against the pain this world inflicted on the unwary.

Yet, as he approached the motel on this hot Montana summer morning, Killian felt an oblique spark of interest that he hated to admit. Susannah was a melodic name, suggestive of someone with sensitivity. Was she? What color was her hair? What color were her eyes? Killian could read a person's soul through the eyes. That ability to delve into people, to know them inside out, was his greatest strength. On the flip side, he allowed no one to know him. Even Morgan Trayhern, who had one of the most sophisticated security companies in America, had only a very thin background dossier on him. And Killian wanted it kept that way. He wanted no one to know the extent of the pain he carried within him—or what he'd done about it. That kind of information could be ammunition for his enemies—and could mean danger to anyone close to him. Still, his mind dwelled on the enigmatic Susannah Anderson. She could be in more danger with Killian around than from any potential hit man. Why couldn't Morgan understand that? Killian hadn't wanted to tell Morgan his reasons for refusing to take assignments involving women; he'd never told anyone. A frown worked its way across his brow. Susannah had been a victim of violence, just like Meg. More than likely, she was afraid of everything.

Arriving at his motel room, Killian methodically packed the essentials he traveled with: a long, wicked-looking hunting knife, the nine-millimeter Beretta that he wore beneath his left armpit in a shoulder holster, and his dark brown leather coat.

When he'd placed a few other necessary items in a beat-up leather satchel, Killian was ready for his next assignment. He'd never been to Kentucky, so he'd have a new area to explore. But whether he wanted to or not, he had to meet Susannah Anderson. The thought tied his gut into painful knots. Damn Morgan's stubbornness! The woman was better off without Killian around. How in the hell was he going to handle his highly volatile emotions, not to mention her?

Chapter One

"We're so glad you've come," Pansy Anderson gushed as she handed Killian a cup of coffee and sat down at the kitchen table across from him.

Killian gave the woman a curt nod. The trip to Glen, Kentucky, and from there to the fruit farm, had passed all too quickly. However, the Andersons' warm welcome had dulled some of his apprehension. Ordinarily, Killian spoke little, but this woman's kindness made his natural reticence seem rude. Leathery-looking Sam Anderson sat at his elbow, work-worn hands clutching a chipped ceramic mug of hot black coffee. Pansy, who appeared to be in her sixties, was thin, with a face that spoke of a harsh outdoor life.

As much as Killian wanted to be angry at everyone, he knew these people didn't deserve his personal frustration. Struggling with emotions he didn't dare explore, Killian whispered tautly, "I'm glad to be here, Mrs. Anderson." It was an utter lie, but still, when he looked into Pansy's worn features he saw relief and hope in her eyes. He scowled inwardly at her reaction. He couldn't offer hope to them or to their daughter. More likely, he presented a danger equal to the possibility of the murderer's coming after Susannah. Oh, God, what was he going to do? Killian's gut clenched with anxiety.

"Call me Pansy." She got up, wiping her hands on her red apron. "I think it's so nice of Morgan to send you here for a rest. To tell you the truth, we could sure use company like yours after what happened to our Susannah." She went to the kitchen counter and began peeling potatoes for the evening meal. "Pa, you think Susannah might like the company?"

"Dunno, Ma. Maybe." Sam's eyes became hooded, and he stared down at his coffee, pondering her question. "My boy, Dennis, served with Morgan. Did he tell you that?"

"No, he didn't."

"That's right—in Vietnam. Dennis died up there on that hill with everyone else. My son sent glowing letters back about Captain Trayhern." Sam looked up. "To this day, I've kept those letters. It helps ease the pain I feel when I miss Denny."

Pansy sighed. "We call Susannah our love baby, Killian. She was born shortly after Denny was killed. She sure plugged up a hole in our hearts. She was such a beautiful baby...."

"Now, Ma," Sam warned gruffly, "don't go getting teary-eyed on us. Susannah's here and, thank the good Lord above, she's alive." Sam turned his attention to Killian. "We need to warn you about our daughter. Since she came back to us from the coma, she's been actin' awful strange."

"Before the tragedy," Pansy added, "Susannah was always such a lively, outgoing young woman. She's a teacher over at the local grade school in Glen. The mentally and physically handicapped children are her first love. She used to laugh, dance, and play beautiful music." Pansy gestured toward the living room of the large farmhouse. "There's a piano in there, and Susannah can play well. Now she never touches it. If she hears music, she runs out of the house crying."

"And she don't want anything to do with anyone. Not even us, much of the time," Sam whispered. He gripped the cup hard, his voice low with feeling. "Susannah is the kindest, most loving daughter on the face of this earth, Killian. She wouldn't harm a fly. She cries if one of Ma's baby chicks dies. When you meet her, you'll see what we're saying."

"The violence has left her disfigured in a kind of invisible way," Pansy said. "She has nasty headaches, the kind that make her throw up. They come on when she's under stress. She hasn't gone back to teach, because she hasn't found her voice yet. The doctors say the loss of her voice isn't due to the blow on her head."

"It's mental," Sam added sadly.

"Yes . . . I suppose it is . . . ." Pansy admitted softly.

"It's emotional," Killian rasped, "not mental." He was instantly sorry he'd spoken, as both of them gave him a strange look. Shifting in his chair, Killian muttered, "I know someone who experienced something similar." Meg had never lost her voice, but he'd suffered with her, learning plenty about emotional wounds. He saw the relief in their faces, and the shared hope. Dammit, they shouldn't hope! Killian clamped his mouth shut and scowled deeply, refusing to meet their eyes.

Pansy rattled on, blotting tears from her eyes. "You understand, then."

Pansy gave him a wobbly smile and wiped her hands off on the towel hanging up on a hook next to the sink. "We just don't know, Killian. Susannah writes us notes so we can talk with her that way. But if we try and ask her about the shooting she runs away, and we don't see her for a day or two."

"She's out in the old dilapidated farmhouse on the other side of the orchard—but not by our choice," Sam offered unhappily. "That was the old family homestead for over a hundred years 'fore my daddy built this place. When Susannah came home from the hospital last month, she insisted on moving into that old, broken-down house. No one's lived there for twenty years or more! It's about half a mile across the hill from where we live now. We had to move her bed and fetch stuff out to her. Sometimes, on a good day, she'll come join us for supper. Otherwise, she makes her own meals and stays alone over there. It's as if she wants to hide from the world—even from us...."

Killian nodded, feeling the pain that Pansy and Sam carried for their daughter. As the silence in the kitchen became stilted, Killian forced himself to ask a few preliminary questions. "How old is Susannah?"

Sam roused himself. "Going on twenty-seven."

"And you say she's a teacher?"

A proud smile wreathed Pansy's features as she washed dishes in the sink. "Yes, she's a wonderful teacher! Do you know, she's the only member of either of our families that got a college degree? The handicapped children love her so much. She taught art class." With a sigh, Pansy added, "Lordy, she won't paint or draw anymore, either."

"Nope," Sam said. "All she does is work in the orchard, garden and tend the animals—mostly the sick ones. That's what seems to make her feel safe."

"And she goes for long walks alone," Pansy added. "I worry. She knows these hills well, but there's this glassy look that comes into her eyes, Killian, and I sometimes wonder if she realizes where she's at."

"Have there been any strangers around, asking about Susannah?" Killian asked offhandedly. Now he understood why Morgan didn't want to tell these gentle, simple people the truth of the situation. But how the hell was he going to balance everything and keep a professional attitude?

"Oh," Pansy said with a laugh, "we get lots of folks up here to buy our fruits, nuts and fresh garden vegetables. And I'm known for my healin' abilities, so we always have folks stoppin' by. That's somethin' Susannah took to—using herbs to heal people with. She's a good healer, and the hill folk, if they can't get to me because I'm busy, they'll go to Susannah. We have a huge herb garden over by the old homestead, and she's making our medicines for this year as the herbs are ready for pickin'."

"That and using white lightning to make tinctures from those herbs." Sam chuckled. And then he raised his bushy eyebrows. "I make a little corn liquor on the side. Strictly for medicinal purposes." He grinned.

Killian nodded, reading between the lines. Although the Andersons were farm people, they were well-off by hill standards. When he'd driven up earlier in the brown Land Cruiser he'd rented at the airport, he'd noted that the rolling green hills surrounding the large two-story white farmhouse were covered with orchards. He'd also seen a large chicken coop, and at least two hundred chickens roaming the hundred acres, ridding the land of insect pests. He'd seen a couple of milking cows, a flock of noisy gray geese, some wild mallards that made their home in a nearby pond, and a great blue heron walking along the edge of the water, probably hunting frogs. In Killian's mind, this place was perfect for someone like him, someone who was world-weary and in need of some genuine rest.

"Why don't you go out and meet Susannah?" Pansy asked hopefully. "You should introduce yourself. Maybe what she needs is someone her own age to get on with. That might help her heal."

White-hot anger clashed with gut-wrenching fear within Killian. Anger at Morgan for forcing him to take this mission. Fear of what he might do around Susannah if he didn't maintain tight control over his emotions. Killian kept his expression passive. Struggling to keep his voice noncommittal, he said, "Yes, I'll meet your daughter. But don't get your hopes up about anything happening." His tone came out harder than he'd anticipated. "I'm here for a rest, Mrs. Anderson. I'm a man of few words, and I like to be left alone."

Pansy's face fell a little, but she quickly summoned up a soft smile. "Why, of course, Mr. Killian. You are our guest, and we want you to feel free to come and go as you please."

Kindness was something Killian had *never* been able to deal with. He stood abruptly, the scraping of the wooden chair against the yellowed linoleum floor an irritant to his taut nerves. "I don't intend to be lazy. I'll help do some work around the place while I'm here."

"I can always use a pair of extra hands," Sam said, "and I'd be beholden to you for that."

Relief swept through Killian, at least momentarily. Work would help keep him away from Susannah. Yet, as a bodyguard, he'd have to remain alert and nearby—even if it was the last thing he wanted to do. But work would also help him get to know the farm and its layout, to anticipate where a threat to Susannah might come from.

Sam rose to his full six-foot-five-inch height. He was as thin as a spring sapling. "Come meet our daughter, Mr. Killian. Usually, this time of day, she's out in the herb garden. It's best I go with you. Otherwise, she's liable to start 'cause you're a stranger."

"Of course," Killian said. Everything about the Anderson home spoke of stark simplicity, he noted as he followed Sam. The floors were covered with linoleum, worn but clean, and lovingly polished. The handmade furniture looked antique, no doubt crafted by Anderson men over the generations. A green crocheted afghan covered the back of the sofa. Pansy had mentioned when he arrived that it had been made by her mother, who had recently passed away at the age of ninety-eight. Evidently, a long-lived family, Killian mused as he followed Sam out the creaky screen door onto the large wooden porch, where a swing hung.

"Now," Sam warned him, "don't take offense if Susannah sees you and takes off for her house. Sometimes when folks come to buy our produce they mistakenly stop at the old house. She locks herself in and won't go near the door."

Not a bad idea, Killian thought, with her assailant still on the prowl. Sometimes paranoia could serve a person well, he ruminated. He looked at himself. He was paranoid, too, but with good cause. As they walked down a well-trodden path lined with fruit trees he wondered how much Susannah knew of her own situation.

"Now," Sam was saying as he took long, slow strides, "this here's the apple orchard. We got mostly Gravestein and Jonathan varieties, 'cause folks are always lookin' for good pie apples." He gestured to the right. "Over there is the Bartlett pears and Bing cherries and sour cherries. To the left, we got Alberta and freestone peaches. Ma loves figs, so we got her a row of them, too. Susannah likes the nut trees, so I ended up planting about twenty acres of black walnuts. Darn good taste to the things, but they come in this thick outer shell, and you have to wait till it dries before you can even get to the nut. It's a lot of work, but Susannah, as a kid, used to sit around for hours, shelling those things by the bucketful. The black are the best-tasting of all walnuts."

Killian nodded, his gaze never still. The surrounding rolling hills, their trees bearing nearly mature fruit, looked idyllic. A variety of birds flew through the many branches and he heard babies cheeping loudly for their parents to bring them food. Still, the serene orchard was forestlike, offering easy cover for a hit man.

After about a fifteen-minute walk up a gentle slope, Killian halted beside Sam where the orchard opened up into an oblong meadow of grass. In the center of the open area stood an old shanty with a rusted tin roof. The sides of the ramshackle house were grayed from years of weathering, and several windows needed to be repaired, their screens torn or rusted or missing altogether. Killian glanced over at Sam in surprise.

"I told you before—Susannah insists upon living in this place. Why, I don't know," Sam muttered. "It needs a heap of fixin' to be livable, if you ask me." He stuffed his hands into the pockets of his coveralls. "Come on. The herb garden is on the other side of the house."

Susannah sank her long fingers into the welcoming black warmth of the fertile soil. Then, taking a clump of chives, she placed it in the hole she'd dug. The inconstant breeze was dying down now that dusk had arrived. She heard the singing of the birds, a peaceful reminder that no one was nearby. A red-breasted robin flew to the white picket fence that enclosed the large herb garden. Almost immediately he began to chirp excitedly, fluttering his wings.

It was a warning. Susannah quickly looked around, feeling vulnerable with her back turned toward whoever was approaching. Her father rounded the corner of the house, then her heart began beating harder. There was a stranger—a man—with him.

Ordinarily Susannah would have run, but in an instant the man's steely blue gaze met and held her own, and something told her to stay where she was. Remaining on her knees in the soil, Susannah watched their progress toward her.

The man's catlike eyes held on hers, but instead of the naked fear she usually felt at a stranger's approach since coming out of the coma, Susannah felt an odd sizzle of apprehension. But what kind? His face was hard-looking, revealing no hint of emotion in his eyes or the set of his mouth. His hair was black and military-short, and his skin was deeply bronzed by the sun. Her heart started to hammer in warning.

Her father greeted her with a smile. "Susannah, I've brought a friend to introduce to you. Come on, honey, come over and meet him."

The stranger's oddly opaque gaze held her suspended. Susannah gulped convulsively and set the chives aside. Her fingers were stained dark from the soil, and the jeans she wore were thick with dust. Slowly, beneath his continued inspection, Susannah forced herself to her bare feet. The power of the stranger's gaze, the anger she saw in the depths of his eyes, held her captive.

"Susannah?" Sam prodded gently as he halted at the gate and opened it. "Honey, he won't hurt you. Come on over...."

"No," Killian said, his voice hoarse. "Let her be. Let her get used to me."

Sam gave him a quizzical look, but said nothing.

Killian wasn't breathing. Air seemed to have jammed in his chest. Susannah was more than beautiful; she was ethereal. Her straight sable-colored hair flowed around her slender form, almost touching her breasts. Her simple white cotton blouse and jeans enhanced her figure. Killian could see no outward signs of the violence she'd endured, although at some point in her life her nose had been broken. The bump was prominent, and he wondered about the story behind it. Her lips were full, and slightly parted now. But it was her eyes—large, expressive, dove gray—that entranced him the most.

Who is he? Why is he looking at me like that? Susannah looked down at herself. Sure, her jeans were dirty, but she had been gardening all day. Her feet, too, were covered with soil. Automatically she raised a hand to touch the front of her blouse. Was one of her buttons undone? No. Again she raised her head and met those eyes that, though emotionless, nonetheless drew her. There was a sense of armor around him that startled her. A hard, impervious shell of self-protection. She'd often sensed the same quality around her handicapped children when they first started school—a need to protect themselves against the all-too-common hurts they were subjected to. But there was more than that to this man's bearing, Susannah realized as she allowed her intuition to take over. She also sensed a darkness, a sadness, around this tall, lean man, who was probably in his mid-thirties. He felt edgy to her, and it set her on edge, too. Who was he? Another police detective from Lexington, come to grill her? To try to jar loose her frozen memory? Susannah's hands grew damp with apprehension. This man frightened her in a new and unknown way. Maybe it was that unexpected anger banked in his eyes.

Killian used all his senses, finely honed over years of dangerous work, to take in Susannah. He saw her fine nostrils quiver and flare, as if she were a wary young deer ready for flight. He felt the fear rise around her, broadcast in every line of her tension-held body. Meg's once-beautiful face floated in front of him. The terror he'd felt as he stood at her hospital bedside as she became conscious for the first time since the blast slammed back into him. Smiling didn't come easily to him, but he'd forced one then for Meg's benefit, and it had made all the difference in the world. She'd reached out and weakly gripped his hand and begun to cry, but to Killian it had been a good sign, a sign that she wanted to live.

Now, for Susannah's benefit, Killian forced the corners of his mouth upward as he saw terror come to her widening eyes. Although he was angry at Morgan, he didn't need to take it out on her. Almost instantly he saw the tension on her face dissipate.

Fighting the screaming awareness of his emotional response to Susannah, Killian said to Sam in a low voice, "Go ahead and make the introduction, and then leave us. I don't think she's going to run."

Scratching his head, Sam nodded. "Darned if I don't believe you. For some reason, she ain't as afraid of you as all the rest."

Killian barely nodded as he continued to hold Susannah's assessing stare. Her arms were held tightly at her sides. Her fingers were long and artistic-looking. She seemed more like a girl in her teens—barefoot and in touch with the magic of the Earth—than a schoolteacher of twenty-seven.

"Honey, this is Mr. Killian," Sam said gently to his daughter. "He's a friend of Morgan's, come to stay with us and rest up for a month or so. Ma and I said he could stay. He's a friend, honey. Not a stranger. Do you understand?"

Susannah nodded slowly, never taking her eyes off Killian.

What is your first name? The words were there, on the tip of her tongue, but they refused to be given voice. Frustration thrummed through Susannah. How she ached to speak again—but some invisible hand held her tongue-tied. Killian's mouth had curved into the barest of smiles, sending an odd heat sheeting through her. Shaken by his presence, Susannah could only nod, her hands laced shyly together in front of her. Still, she was wary. It wasn't something she could just automatically turn off.

Killian was excruciatingly uncomfortable, and he wanted to get the social amenities over with. "Thanks, Sam," he said brusquely.

Sam's gaze moved from his daughter to Killian and back to her. "Honey, supper's in a hour. Ma would like you to join us. Will you?"

Susannah felt her heartbeat picking up again, beating wildly with apprehension over this man named Killian—a male stranger who had come to disrupt the silent world where she'd retreated to be healed. She glanced down at her feet and then lifted her chin.

I don't know. I don't know, Pa. Let me see how I feel. Susannah was disappointed with herself. All she could do was shrug delicately. Ordinarily she carried a pen and paper with her in order to communicate with her folks, or friends of the family who stopped to visit. But today, not expecting visitors, she'd left her pad and pen back at the house.

"Good enough," Sam told her gruffly. "Maybe you'll let Killian walk you back afterward."

Killian stood very still after Sam disappeared. He saw the nervousness and curiosity reflected in Susannah's wide eyes—and suddenly he almost grinned at the irony of their situation. He was normally a person of few words, and for the first time in his life he was going to have to carry the conversation. He spread his hand out in a gesture of peace.

"I hope I didn't stop you from planting."

No, you didn't. Susannah glanced sharply down at the chives. She knelt and began to cover the roots before they dried out. As she worked, she keyed her hearing to where the man stood, outside the gate. Every once in a while, she glanced up. Each time she did, he was still standing there, motionless, hands in the pockets of his jeans, an old, beat-up leather jacket hanging loosely on his lean frame. His serious features were set, and she sensed an unhappiness radiating from him. About what? Being here? Meeting her? So many things didn't make sense to her. If he was one of Morgan's friends, why would he be unhappy about being here? If he was here for a vacation, he should be relaxed.

Killian caught Susannah's inquiring gaze. Then, dusting off her hands, she continued down the row, pulling weeds. The breeze gently blew strands of her thick hair across her shoulders, framing her face.

Although he hadn't moved, Killian's eyes were active, sizing up the immediate vicinity—the possible entrances to the shanty and the layout of the surrounding meadow. His gaze moved back to Susannah, who continued acting guarded, nearly ignoring him. She was probably hoping he'd go away and leave her alone, he thought wryly. God knew, he'd like to do exactly that. His anger toward Morgan grew in volume.

"I haven't seen a woman in bare feet since I left Ireland," he finally offered in a low, clipped tone. No, conversation wasn't his forte.

Susannah stopped weeding and jerked a look in his direction. Killian crossed to sit on the grassy bank, his arms around his knees, his gaze still on her.

As if women can't go with their shoes off!

Killian saw the disgust in her eyes. Desperately he cast about for some way to lessen the tension between them. As long as she distrusted him, he wouldn't be able to get close enough to protect her. Inwardly Killian cursed Morgan.

Forcing himself to try again, he muttered, "That wasn't an insult. Just an observation. My sister, Meg, who's about your age, always goes barefoot in the garden, too." He gestured toward the well-kept plants. "Looks like you give them a lot of attention. Meg always said plants grew best when you gave them love." Just talking about Meg, even to this wary, silent audience of one, eased some of his pain for his sister.

You know how I feel! Weeds in her hands, Susannah straightened, surprised by the discovery. Killian had seen her facial expression and read it accurately. Hope rushed through her. Her mother and father, as dearly as they loved her, couldn't seem to read her feelings at all since she'd come out of the coma. But suddenly this lanky, tightly coiled stranger with the sky-blue eyes, black hair and soft, hesitant smile could.

Are you a psychiatrist? I hope not. Susannah figured she'd been through enough testing to last her a lifetime. Older men with glasses and beards had pronounced her hysterical due to her trauma and said it was the reason she couldn't speak. Her fingers tightened around the weeds as she stood beneath Killian's cool, expressionless inspection.

Killian saw the tension in Susannah's features dissolve for just an instant. He'd touched her, and he knew it. Frustrated and unsure of her reaction to him, he tried again, but his voice came out cold. "Weeds make good compost. Do you have a compost pile around here?"

Susannah looked intensely at this unusual man, feeling him instead of listening to his words, which he seemed to have mouthed in desperation. Ordinarily, if she'd met Killian on a busy street, he would have frightened her. His face was lean, like the rest of him, and his nose was large and straight, with a good space between his slightly arched eyebrows. There was an intense alertness in those eyes that reminded her of a cougar. And although he had offered that scant smile initially, his eyes contained a hardness that Susannah had never seen in her life. Since the incident that had changed her life, she had come to rely heavily on her intuitive abilities to ferret out people's possible ulterior motives toward her. The hospital therapist had called it paranoia. But in this case, Susannah sensed that a great sadness had settled around Killian like a cloak. And danger.

Why danger? And is it danger to me? He did *look* dangerous, there was no doubt. Susannah couldn't find one telltale sign in his features of humanity or emotion. But her fear warred with an image she couldn't shake, the image of the sad but crooked smile that had made him appear vulnerable for one split second out of time.

Chapter Two

Killian watched Susannah walk slowly and cautiously through the garden gate. She was about three feet away from him now, and he probed her for signs of wariness. He had no wish to minimize her guardedness toward him—if he could keep her at arm's length and do his job, this assignment might actually work out. If he couldn't...

Just the way Susannah moved snagged a sharp stab of longing deep within him. She had the grace of a ballet dancer, her hips swaying slightly as she stepped delicately across the rows of healthy plants. He decided not to follow her, wanting to allow her more time to adjust to his presence. Just then a robin, sitting on the fence near Killian, took off and landed in the top of an old, gnarled apple tree standing alone just outside the garden. Instantly there was a fierce cheeping, and Killian cocked his head to one side. A half-grown baby robin was perched precariously on the limb near the nest, fluttering his wings demandingly as the parent hovered nearby with food in his beak.

Killian sensed Susannah's presence and slowly turned his head. She was standing six feet away, watching him pointedly. There was such beauty in her shadowed gray eyes. Killian recognized that shadow— Meg's eyes were marred by the same look.

"That baby robin is going to fall off that limb if he isn't careful."

Yes, he is. Yesterday he did, and I had to pick him up and put him back in the tree. Frustrated by her inability to speak the words, Susannah nodded and wiped her hands against her thighs. Once again she found herself wanting her notepad and pen. He was a stranger and couldn't be trusted, a voice told her. Still, he was watching the awkward progress of the baby robin with concern.

Unexpectedly the baby robin shrieked. Susannah opened her mouth to cry out, but only a harsh, strangulated sound came forth as the small bird fluttered helplessly down through the branches of the apple tree and hit the ground roughly, tumbling end over end. When the baby regained his composure, he began to scream for help, and both parents flew around and around him.

Without thinking, Susannah rushed past Killian to rescue the bird, as she had yesterday.

"No," Killian whispered, reaching out to stop Susannah. "I'll do it." Her skin was smooth and sunwarmed beneath his fingers, and instantly Killian released her, the shock of the touch startling not only him, but her, too.

Susannah gasped, jerking back, her mouth opened in shock. Her skin seemed to tingle where his fingers had briefly, carefully grasped her wrist.

Taken aback by her reaction, Killian glared at her, then immediately chastised himself. After all, didn't he want her to remain fearful of him? Inside, though, his heart winced at the terror he saw in her gaze, at the contorted shape of her lips as she stared up at him—as if he was her assailant. His action had been rash, he thought angrily. Somehow Susannah's presence had caught him off guard. Infuriated by his own blind reactions, Killian stood there at a loss for words.

Susannah saw disgust in Killian's eyes, and then, on its heels, a gut-wrenching sadness. Still stunned by his swift touch, she backed even farther away from him. Finally the robin's plaintive cheeping impinged on her shocked senses, and she tore her attention from Killian, pointing at the baby robin now hopping around on the ground.

"Yeah. Okay, I'll get the bird," Killian muttered crossly. He was furious with himself, at the unexpected emotions that brief touch had aroused. For the most fleeting moment, his heart jumped at the thought of what it would feel like to kiss Susannah until she was breathless with need of him. Thoroughly disgusted that the thought had even entered his head, Killian moved rapidly to rescue the baby bird. What woman would be interested in him? He was a dark introvert of a man, given to very little communication. A man haunted by a past that at any moment could avalanche into his present and effectively destroy a woman who thought she might care for him. No, he was dangerous—a bomb ready to explode—and he was damned if he was going to put any woman in the line of fire.

As he leaned down and trapped the robin carefully between his hands, the two parents flew overhead, shrieking, trying to protect their baby. Gently Killian cupped the captured baby, lifting the feathered tyke and staring into his shiny black eyes.

"Next time some cat might find you first and think you're a tasty supper," he warned sternly as he turned toward the apple tree. Placing the bird in his shirt pocket, he grabbed a low branch and began to climb.

Susannah stood below, watching Killian's lithe progress. Everything about the man was methodical. He never stepped on a weak limb; he studied the situation thoroughly before placing each foot to push himself upward toward the nest. Yet, far from plodding, he had an easy masculine grace.

Killian settled the robin in its nest and quickly made his way down to avoid the irate parents. Leaping the last few feet, he landed with the grace of a large cat. "Well, our good deed is done for the day," he said gruffly, dusting off his hands.

His voice was as icy as his unrelenting features, and Susannah took another step away from him.

Thank you for rescuing the baby. But how can such a hard man perform such a gentle feat? What's your story, Killian? His eyes turned impatient under her inspection, and Susannah tore her gaze away from him. The man had something to hide, it seemed.

How much more do you know about me? What did my folks tell you? Susannah felt an odd sort of shame at the thought of Killian knowing what had happened to her. Humiliation, too, coupled with anger and fear—the entire gamut of feelings she'd lived with daily since the shooting. Out of nervousness, she raised a hand to her cheek, which felt hot and flushed.

Killian noted the hurt in Susannah's eyes as she self-consciously brushed her cheek with her fingertips. And in that moment he saw the violence's lasting damage: loss of self-esteem. She was afraid of him, and part of him ached at the unfairness of it, but he accepted his fate bitterly. Let Susannah think him untrustworthy—dangerous. Those instincts might save her life, should her assailant show up for another try at killing her.

"I need to wash my hands," he said brusquely, desperate to break the tension between them. He had to snap out of it. He couldn't afford to allow her to affect him—and possibly compromise his ability to protect her from a killer.

Unexpectedly Susannah felt tears jam into her eyes. She stood there in abject surprise as they rolled down her cheeks, unbidden, seemingly tapped from some deep source within her. Why was she crying? She hadn't cried since coming out of the coma! Embarrassed that Killian was watching her, a disgruntled look on his face, Susannah raised trembling hands to her cheeks.

Killian swayed—and caught himself. Every fiber of his being wanted to reach out and comfort Susannah. The tears, small, sun-touched crystals, streamed down her flushed cheeks. The one thing he couldn't bear was to see a woman cry. A weeping child he could handle, but somehow, when a woman cried, it was different.

Different, and gut-wrenchingly disturbing. Meg's tears had torn him apart, her cries shredding what was left of his feelings.

Looking down at Susannah now, Killian felt frustration and disgust at his inability to comfort her. But that edge, that distrust, had to stay in place if he was to do his job.

Turning away abruptly, he looked around for a garden hose, for anything, really, that would give him an excuse to escape her nearness. Spying a hose leading from the side of the house, he turned on his heel and strode toward the faucet. Relief flowed through him as he put distance between them, the tightened muscles in his shoulders and back loosening. Trying to shake pangs of guilt for abandoning her, Killian leaned down and turned on the faucet. He washed his hands rapidly, then wiped them on the thighs of his jeans as he straightened.

He glanced back toward Susannah who still stood near the garden, looking alone and unprotected. As he slowly walked back to where she stood, he thrust his hands into the pockets of his jeans. "It's almost time for dinner," he said gruffly. "I'm hungry. Are you coming?"

Susannah felt hollow inside. The tears had left her terribly vulnerable, and right now she needed human company more than usual. Killian's harsh company felt abrasive to her in her fragile emotional state, and she knew she'd have to endure walking through the orchard to her folks' house with him. She forced herself to look into his dark, angry features. This mute life of pad and pencil was unbelievably frustrating. Normally she believed mightily in communicating and confronting problems, and without a voice, it was nearly impossible to be herself. The old Susannah would have asked Killian what his problem with her was. Instead she merely gestured for him to follow her.

Killian maintained a discreet distance from Susannah as they wound their way through the orchard on the well-trodden path. He wanted to ask Susannah's forgiveness for having abandoned her earlier—to explain why he had to keep her at arm's length. But then he laughed derisively at himself. Susannah would never understand. No woman would. He noticed that as they walked Susannah's gaze was never still, constantly searching the area, as if she were expecting to be attacked. It hurt him to see her in that mode. The haunted look in her eyes tore at him. Her beautiful mouth was pursed, the corners drawn taut, as if she expected a blow at any moment.

Not while I'm alive will another person ever *harm you,* he promised grimly. Killian slowed his pace, baffled at the intensity of the feeling that came with the thought. The sun shimmered through the leaves of the fruit trees, scattering light across the green grass in a patchwork-quilt effect, touching Susannah's hair and bringing red highlights to life, intermixed with threads of gold. Killian wondered obliquely if she had some Irish blood in her.

In the Andersons' kitchen, Killian noted the way Susannah gratefully absorbed her mother's obvious care and genuine concern. He watched the sparkle come back to her lovely gray eyes as Pansy doted over her. Susannah had withdrawn into herself on their walk to the farmhouse. Now Killian watched her re-emerge from that private, silent world, coaxed out by touches and hugs from her parents.

He'd made her retreat, and he felt like hell about it. But there could be no ambiguity about his function here at the farm. Sitting at the table now, his hand around a mug of steaming coffee, Killian tried to protect himself against the emotional warmth that pervaded the kitchen. The odors of home-cooked food, fresh and lovingly prepared, reminded him of a far gentler time in his life, the time when he was growing up in Ireland. There hadn't been many happy times in Killian's life, but that had been one—his mother doting over him and Meg, the lighthearted lilt of her laughter, the smell of fresh bread baking in the oven, her occasional touch upon his shoulder or playful ruffling of his hair. Groaning, he blindly gulped his coffee, and nearly burned his mouth in the process.

Susannah washed her hands at the kitchen sink, slowly dried them, and glanced apprehensively over at Killian. He sat at the table like a dark, unhappy shadow, his hand gripping the coffee mug. She was trying to understand him, but it was impossible. Her mother smiled at him, and tried to cajole a hint of a reaction from Killian, but he seemed impervious to human interaction.

As Pansy served the dinner, Killian tried to ignore the fact that he was seated opposite Susannah. She had an incredible ability to communicate with just a glance from those haunting eyes. Killian held on tightly to his anger at the thought that she had almost died.

"Why, you're lookin' so much better," Pansy gushed to her daughter as she placed mashed potatoes, spareribs and a fresh garden salad on the table.

Susannah nodded and smiled for her mother's sake. Just sitting across from Killian was unnerving. But because she loved her mother and father fiercely she was trying to ignore Killian's cold, icy presence and act normally.

Sam smiled and passed his daughter the platter of ribs. "Do you think you'll get along with Killian hereabouts for a while?"

Susannah felt Killian's eyes on her and refused to look up, knowing that he was probably studying her with the icy gaze of a predator for his intended victim. She glanced over at her father, whose face was open and readable, and found the strength somewhere within herself to lie. A white lie, Susannah told herself as she forced a smile and nodded.

Killian ate slowly, allowing his senses to take in the cheerful kitchen and happy family setting. The scents of barbecued meat and thick brown gravy and the tart smell of apples baking in the oven were sweeter than any perfume.

"I don't know what you did," Pansy told Killian, "but whatever it is, Susannah looks so much better! Doesn't she, Sam?"

Spooning gravy onto a heaping portion of mashed potatoes, Sam glanced up. "Ma, you know how uncomfortable Susannah gets when we talk as if she's not here."

Chastened, Pansy smiled. "I'm sorry, dear," she said, giving her daughter a fond look and a pat on the arm in apology.

Susannah wondered glumly how she could possibly look better with Killian around. Without a doubt, the man made her uncomfortable. She decided it was just that her mother wanted to see her looking better. Aching inwardly, Susannah thought how terribly the past three months had worn down her folks. They had both aged noticeably, and it hurt her to realize that her stupid, failed foray into the "big" world outside Kentucky had cost them, too. If only she hadn't been so naive about the world, it might not have happened, and her parents might not have had to suffer this way. Luckily, her school insurance had covered the massive medical bills; Susannah knew her folks would have sold the farm, if necessary, to help her cover expenses.

"Let's talk about you, Killian," Pansy said brightly, turning the conversation to him.

Killian saw Susannah's eyes suddenly narrow upon him, filled with curiosity—and some indefinable emotion that set his pulse to racing. He hesitated, not wanting to sound rude. "Ordinarily, Pansy, I don't open up to anyone."

"Whatever for?"

Sam groaned. "Honey, the man's got a right to some privacy, don't he?"

Pansy laughed. "Now, Pa..."

Clearing his throat, Killian moved the mashed potatoes around on his blue-and-white plate. He realized he wasn't going to be able to get around Pansy's good-natured probing. "I work in the area of high security." The explanation came out gruffly—a warning, he hoped, for her to stop asking questions.

"Surely," Pansy said, with a gentle laugh, "you can tell me if you're married or not. Or about your family?"

Tension hung in the air. Killian put down his fork, keeping a tight rein on his reaction to what he knew was a well-intentioned question. Sam shot him an apologetic look that spoke volumes, but Killian also saw Susannah's open interest. She'd stopped eating, and was waiting to hear his answer.

Killian felt heat creeping up his neck and into his cheeks. Pain at the memory of his family sheared through him. He dropped his gaze to the uneaten food on his plate and felt an avalanche of unexpected grief that seemed to suck the life out of him momentarily. Unwillingly he looked up—and met Susannah's compassionate gaze.

Killian shoved his chair back, and the scraping sound shattered the tension. "Excuse me," he rasped, "I'm done eating."

Susannah saw pain in Killian's eyes and heard the roughness of emotion in his voice as he moved abruptly to his feet. The chair nearly tipped over backward, but he caught it in time. Without a sound, Killian stalked from the kitchen.

"Oh, dear," Pansy whispered, her fingers against her lips. "I didn't mean to upset him...."

Susannah reached out and gripped her mother's hand. She might not be able to talk, but she could at least offer the reassurance of touch.

Sam cleared his throat. "Ma, he's a closed kind of man. Didn't you see that?"

Pansy shrugged weakly and patted her daughter's hand. "Oh, I guess I did, Sam, but you know me— I'm such a busybody. Maybe I should go after him and apologize."

"Just let him be, Ma, and he'll come around," Sam counseled gently.

"I don't know," Pansy whispered, upset. "When I asked him about his family, did you see his face?"

Susannah nodded and released her mother's hand. As she continued to finish her meal, she ruminated on that very point. Killian had reacted violently to the question, anguished pain momentarily shadowing his eyes. Susannah had found herself wanting to reach out and reassure him that all would be well. But would it?

Morosely Susannah forced herself to finish eating her dinner. Somehow she wanted to let her mother know that there had been nothing wrong with her questions to Killian. As she had so many times these past months, she wished she could talk. Pansy was just a warm, chatty person by nature, but Susannah understood Killian's discomfort over such questions. Still, she wanted to try to communicate with Killian. She would use the excuse that he could walk her home, since it would be nearly dark. Her father never allowed her to walk home alone at night. At the same time, Susannah felt fear at being alone with him.

What was there about him that made her want to know him? He was a stranger who'd walked into her life only a few hours ago. The fact that he was Morgan's friend meant something, of course. From what her cousin Laura had told her, she knew that Morgan Trayhern drew only loyal, responsible people to him. Still, they were hard men, mercenaries. Susannah had no experience with mercenaries. In fact, she had very little experience with men in general, and especially with men her own age. She felt she wasn't equal to the task of healing the rift between her mother and Killian, but she knew she had to try. Otherwise, her mother would be a nervous wreck every time Killian sat down to eat. No, something had to be done to calm the troubled waters.

Killian was sitting in the living room, pretending to watch television, when he saw Susannah come out of the kitchen. He barely met her gaze as she walked determinedly toward him with a piece of paper in her hand. He saw uncertainty in her eyes—and something else that he couldn't have defined. Knowing that his abruptness had already caused bad feelings, he tensed as she drew close enough to hand him the note.

Walk me home. Please?

Killian lifted his head and studied her darkly. There was such vulnerability to Susannah—and that was what had nearly gotten her killed. Killian couldn't help but respond to the silent plea in her eyes as she stood waiting for his answer.

Without a word, he crushed the note in his hand, got to his feet and headed toward the door. He would use this excuse to check out her house and the surrounding area. When he opened the door for her, she brushed by him, and he felt himself tense. The sweet, fragrant scent of her perfume momentarily encircled him, and he unconsciously inhaled the subtle scent.

It was dusk, the inky stains across the early-autumn sky telling Killian it would soon be dark. As he slowly walked Susannah back to her house, his ears were tuned in to the twilight for any out-of-the-ordinary sounds. He needed to adjust his senses to the normal sounds of this countryside, anyway. Until then, he would have to be even more alert than normal. There were no unusual odors on the fragrant air, and he couldn't ferret out anything unusual visually as he restlessly scanned the orchard.

When they reached her home, Killian realized that it had no electricity. He stood just inside the door and watched as Susannah lit a hurricane lamp filled with kerosene. She placed one lamp on the wooden table, another on the mantel over the fireplace, and a third in the living room. The floorboards, old and gray, creaked beneath her bare feet as she moved about. Uneasy at how little protection the house afforded against a possible intruder, Killian watched her pull open a drawer of an oak hutch.

Susannah located a notebook and pen and gestured for Killian to come and sit down with her at the table. Mystified, Killian sat down tensely at Susannah's elbow while she wrote on the notepad.

When she'd finished writing, she turned the notepad around so that Killian could read her question. The light from the kerosene lamp cast a soft glow around the deeply shadowed kitchen.

Killian eyed the note. ''Is Killian my first or last name?'' he read aloud. He grimaced and reared back on two legs of the chair. ''It's my last name. Everyone calls me by my last name.''

Susannah made a frustrated sound and penned another note.

What is your first name?

Killian scowled heavily and considered her request. Morgan's orders sounded demandingly in his brain. He was to try to get Susannah to remember what her assailant looked like. If he remained too cool and unresponsive to her, she wouldn't want to try to cooperate with him. Yet to reveal himself would be as good as opening up his horrifying past once again. That had happened once before, with terrible results, and he'd vowed it would never happen again. Dammit, anyway! He rubbed his mouth with his hand, feeling trapped. He had to gain Susannah's cooperation. Her trust.

"Sean," he snarled.

Susannah winced, but determinedly wrote another note.

Who do you allow to call you Sean?

Killian stared at the note. Despite Susannah's obvious softness and vulnerability, for the first time he noticed a look of stubbornness in her eyes. He frowned.

"My mother and sister called me by my first name. Just them," he muttered.

Susannah digested his admission. Maybe he used his last name to prevent people getting close to him. But evidently there were at least two women in his life who could reach inside those armored walls and get to him. There was hope, Susannah decided, if Killian allowed his family to use his first name. But she'd heard the warning in his voice when he'd spoken to her mother. She might be a hill woman, and not as worldly as he was, but surely it wasn't unreasonable to expect good manners—even from a mercenary. She held his blunt stare and felt the fear and anger seething around him. That cold armored cloak was firmly in place.

Grimly Susannah penned another note.

My mother didn't mean to make you uncomfortable. If you can find some way to say something to her to defuse the situation, I'd be grateful. She meant well. She didn't mean to chase you from the dinner table.

Killian stared at her printed note for a long time. The silence thickened. Susannah was right; he'd been wrong in his reaction to the situation. He wished he had the words, a way to explain himself. Frustration overwhelmed him. Looking up, he thought for a moment that he might drown in her compassionate gray gaze. Quirking his mouth, he muttered, "When I go back down tonight, I'll tell her I'm sorry."

Susannah smiled slightly and nodded her head.

Thank you. I know so little of Morgan's men. None of us know anything about mercenaries. I hope you can forgive us, too?

Steeling himself against Susannah's attempt to smooth things over, Killian nodded. "Don't worry about it. There's nothing to forgive." He started to get up, but she made an inarticulate sound and reached out, her hand closing around his arm. Killian froze.

Susannah's lips parted when she saw anguish replace the coldness in Killian's eyes as she touched him.

She hadn't meant to reach out like that; it had been instinctive. Somewhere in her heart, she knew that Killian needed touching—a lot of it. She knew all too well through her work the value of touching, the healing quality of a hand upon a shoulder to give necessary support and courage. Hard as he appeared to be, was Killian really any different? Gazing up through the dim light in the kitchen, she saw the tortured look in his eyes.

Thinking that he was repulsed by her touch, she quickly released him.

Killian slowly sat back, his heart hammering in his chest. It was hell trying to keep his feelings at bay. Whether he liked it or not, he could almost read what Susannah was thinking in her expressive eyes. Their soft gray reminded him of a mourning dove—and she was as gentle and delicate as one.

My folks are simple people, Killian. Pa said you were here for a rest. Is that true? If so, for how long?

Killian felt utterly trapped, and he longed to escape. Morgan was expecting the impossible of him. He didn't have the damnable ability to walk with one foot as a protector and the other foot emotionally far enough away from Susannah to do his job. The patient look on her face only aggravated him.

"I'm between missions," he bit out savagely. "And I want to rest somewhere quiet. I'll try to be a better house guest, okay?"

I know you're uncomfortable around me. I don't expect anything from you. I'll be staying up here most of the time, so you'll have the space to rest.

Absolute frustration thrummed through Killian. This was exactly what he *didn't* want! "Look," he growled, "you don't make me uncomfortable, okay? I know what happened to you, and I'm sorry it happened. I have a sister who—"

Susannah tilted her head as he snapped his mouth shut and glared at her. He wanted to run. It was in every line of his body, and it was in his eyes. The tension in the kitchen had become a tangible thing.

Who? What?

Agitated, Killian shot to his feet. He roamed around the kitchen in the semidarkness, seesawing back and forth about what—if anything—he should tell her. She sat quietly, watching him, without any outward sign of impatience. Running his fingers through his hair, he turned suddenly and pinned her with an angry look.

"My sister, Meg, was nearly killed in a situation not unlike yours," he ground out finally. "She's disfigured for life, and she's scared. She lives alone, like a recluse. I've seen what violence has done to her, so I can imagine what it's done to you." He'd said enough. More than enough, judging from the tears that suddenly were shimmering in Susannah's eyes.

Breathing hard, Killian continued to glare at her, hoping she would give up. He didn't want her asking him any more personal questions. Hell, he hadn't intended to bring up Meg! But something about this woman kept tugging at him, pulling him out of his isolation.

I'm sorry for Meg. For you. I've seen what the violence to me has done to my folks. It's awful. It's forever.

As Killian read the note, standing near the table, his shoulders sagged, and all the anger went out of him. "Yes," he whispered wearily, "violence is wrong. All it does is tear people's lives apart." How well he knew that—in more ways than he ever wanted to admit.

If you're a mercenary, then you're always fighting a war, aren't you?

The truth was like a knife in Killian's clenched gut. He stood, arms at his sides, and hung his head as he pondered her simple question. "Mercenaries work in many capacities," he said slowly. "Some of them are very safe and low-risk. But they do deal with violent situations, too." He lifted his head and threw her a warning look. "The more you do it, the more you become it."

Are you always in dangerous situations?

He picked up the note, then slowly crushed it in his hand. Susannah was getting too close. That just couldn't happen. For her sake, it couldn't. Killian arranged his face into the deadliest look he could muster. "More than anything," he told her in a soft rasp, "you should understand that I'm dangerous to you."

It was all the warning Killian could give her short of telling what had happened when one woman *had* gotten to him, touched his heart, made him feel love. He'd sworn he'd never tell anyone that—not even Meg. And he'd vowed never to let it happen again. Susannah was too special, too vulnerable, for him to allow her to get close to him. But she had a kind of courage that frightened Killian; she had the guts to approach someone like him—someone so wounded that he could never be healed.

"I'll see you tomorrow morning," he said abruptly. He scanned the room closely with one sweeping gaze, then glanced down at her. "Because I'm a mercenary, I'm going to check out your house and the surrounding area. I'll be outside after I make a sweep of the house, and then I'll be staying at your folks' place, in the guest bedroom." He rubbed his jaw as he took in the poor condition of the window, which had no screen and no lock. "If you hear anything, come and get me."

I've been living here the last month and nothing has happened. I'll be okay.

Naiveté at best, Killian thought as he read her note. But he couldn't tell her she was in danger—good old Morgan's orders again. His mouth flattening, he stared across the table into her weary eyes. "If you need help, come and get me. Understand?" As much as he wanted to stay nearby to protect Susannah, Killian knew he couldn't possibly move in with her without a darn good explanation for her and her parents. He was hamstrung. And he didn't want to have to live under Susannah's roof, anyway, for very different reasons. As much as he hated to leave her unprotected at the homestead, for now he had no choice.

At least Susannah would remain safe from him, Killian thought as he studied her darkly. His mind shouted that he'd be absolutely useless sleeping down at the Anderson house if the killer tried to reach her here. But what could he do? Torn, he decided that for tonight, he would sleep at the Andersons' and ponder the problem.

With a bare nod, Susannah took in Killian's vibrating warning. He had told her he was a violent man. She sensed the lethal quality about him, and yet those brief flashes she'd had of him without his defenses in place made her believe that deep down he longed for peace, not war.

Chapter Three

As she bathed and prepared to go to bed, Susannah tried to sift through her jumbled feelings. Killian disturbed her, she decided, more than he frightened her. Somehow she was invisibly drawn to him—to the inner man, not the cold exterior he held up like a shield. She pulled her light knee-length cotton gown over her head and tamed her tangled hair with her fingers. The lamplight cast dancing shadows across the opposite wall of the small bathroom. Ordinarily, catching sight of moving silhouettes caused her to start, but tonight it didn't.

Why? Picking up her clothes, Susannah walked thoughtfully through the silent house, the old planks beneath the thin linoleum floor creaking occasionally. Could Killian's unsettling presence somehow have given her a sense of safety? Even if it was an edgy kind of safety? Despite his glowering and his snappish words, Susannah sensed he would help her if she ever found herself in trouble.

With a shake of her head, Susannah dumped her clothes into a hamper in the small side room and made her way toward the central portion of the two-story house. At least four generations of Andersons had lived here, and that in itself gave her a sense of safety. There was something about the old and the familiar that had always meant tranquility to Susannah, and right now she needed that sense as never before.

She went into the kitchen, where the hurricane lamp still threw its meager light. Pictures drawn in crayon wreathed the walls of the area—fond reminders of her most recent class of children. Last year's class. The pictures suggested hope, and Susannah could vividly recall each child's face as she surveyed the individual drawings. They gave her a sense that maybe her life hadn't been completely shattered after all.

Leaning down, Susannah blew out the flame in the lamp, and darkness cloaked the room, making her suddenly edgy. It had been shadowy the night she'd walked from her bus toward the brightly lit central station—she could remember that clearly. She could recall, too, flashbacks of the man who had been killed in front of her. He'd been sharply dressed, with an engaging smile, and he'd approached her as if she were a longtime friend. She'd trusted him—found him attractive, to be honest. She'd smiled and allowed him to take the large carry-on bag that hung from her shoulder. With a shudder, Susannah tried to block the horrifying end to his brief contact with her. Pressing her fingers against her closed eyes, she felt the first signs of one of the massive migraines that seemed to come and go without much warning begin to stalk her.

As she made her way to her bedroom, at the rear of the house—moving around familiar shapes in the dark—Susannah vaguely wondered why Killian's unexpected presence hadn't triggered one of her crippling headaches. He was dangerous, her mind warned her sharply. He'd told her so himself, in the sort of warning growl a cougar might give an approaching hunter. As she pulled back the crisp white sheet and the worn quilt that served as her bedspread, Susannah's heart argued with her practical mind. Killian must have lived through some terrible, traumatic events to project that kind of iciness. As Susannah slid into bed, fluffed her pillow and closed her eyes, she released a long, ragged sigh. Luckily, sleep always cured her headaches, and she was more tired than usual tonight.

Despite her physical weariness, Susannah saw Killian's hard, emotionless face waver before her closed eyes. There wasn't an iota of gentleness anywhere in his features. Yet, as she searched his stormy dark blue eyes, eyes that shouted to everyone to leave him alone, Susannah felt such sadness around him that tears stung her own eyes. Sniffing, she laughed to herself. How easily touched she was! And how much she missed her children. School had started without her, and she was missing a new class of frightened, unsure charges she knew would slowly come out of their protective shells and begin to reach out and touch life.

Unhappily Susannah thought of the doctors' warnings that it would be at least two months before she could possibly go back to teaching. Her world, as she had known it, no longer existed. Where once she'd been trusting of people, now she was not. Darkness had always been her friend—but now it disturbed her. Forcing herself to shut off her rambling thoughts, Susannah concentrated on sleep. Her last images were of Killian, and the sadness that permeated him.

A distinct click awakened Susannah. She froze beneath the sheet and blanket, listening. Her heart rate tripled, and her mouth grew dry. The light of a first-quarter moon spilled in the open window at the head of her old brass bed. The window's screen had been torn loose years ago and never repaired, Susannah knew. Terror coursed through her as she lay still, her muscles aching with fear.

Another click. Carefully, trying not to make a sound, Susannah lifted her head and looked toward the window opposite her bed. A scream jammed in her throat. The profile of a man was silhouetted against the screen. A cry, rooted deep in her lungs, started up through her. Vignettes of the murderer who had nearly taken her life, a man with a narrow face, small eyes and a crooked mouth, smashed into her. If she hadn't been so frightened, Susannah would have rejoiced at finally recalling his face. But now sweat bathed her, and her nightgown grew damp and clung to her as she gripped the sheet, her knuckles whitening.

Breathing raggedly, she watched with widening eyes as the silhouette moved. It wasn't her imagination! The shriek that had lodged in her chest exploded upward. A sound, a mewling cry fraught with desperation, escaped her contorted lips. *Run!* She had to run!

She had to get to her parents' home, where she'd be safe.

Susannah scrambled out of bed, and her bare feet hit the wooden floorboards hard. Frantically she tore at the bedroom door, which she always locked behind her. Several of her nails broke as she yanked the chain guard off and jerked the door open. Blindly she raced through the living room and the kitchen and charged wildly out the back door. Her bare feet sank into the dew-laden grass as she raced through the meadow. Her breath coming in ragged gulps, she ran with abandon.

The shadows of the trees loomed everywhere about her as she sped onward. As she sobbed for breath, she thought she heard heavy footsteps coming up behind her. Oh, God! No! *Not again!*

Killian jerked awake as someone crashed into the back door of the farmhouse. At the sound of frantic pounding he leaped out of the bed. Wearing only light blue pajama bottoms, he reached for his Beretta. In one smooth, unbroken motion he slid the weapon out of its holster and opened the door. Swiftly he raced from the first-floor guest room, through the gloomy depths of the house, to the rear door, where the pounding continued unabated.

The curtains blocked his view, but Killian knew in his gut it was Susannah. Unlocking the door, he pulled it open.

Susannah stood there, her face twisted in terror, tears coursing down her taut cheeks and her gray eyes huge with fear. Without thinking, he opened his arms to her.

She fell sobbing into his arms, her nightdress damp with perspiration. Killian held her sagging form against him with one hand; in the other was his pistol, safety off, held in position, ready to fire. Susannah's sobs were a mixture of rasps and cries as she clung to him. Killian's eyes narrowed to slits as he dragged her away from the open door, pressing her up against the wall, out of view of any potential attacker. Rapidly he searched the darkened porch beyond the open door, and the nearby orchard. His heart was racing wildly. He was aware of Susannah's soft, convulsing form trapped between him and the wall as he remained a protective barrier for her, in case the killer was nearby. But only moonlight showed in the quiet orchard and the countryside beyond.

Seconds passed, and Killian still could detect no movement. Susannah's sobs and gasps drowned out any chance of hearing a possible assailant. "Easy, colleen," he whispered raggedly, easing away from her. The feel of her trembling body beneath him was playing havoc with his carefully controlled emotions so much so, he'd called her colleen, an Irish endearment. Fighting his need to absorb the softness of her womanly form against him, Killian forced himself away from her. Shaken, he drew her into the kitchen and nudged the door closed with his foot. "Come on, sit down." He coaxed Susannah over to the table and pulled the chair out for her. She collapsed into it, her face filled with terror as she stared apprehensively at the back door. Killian placed a hand on her shoulder, feeling the terrible tension in her.

"It's all right," he told her huskily, standing behind her chair, alert and waiting. The kitchen had only two small windows, just above the counter and sinks, and the table was in a corner, where a shooter wouldn't be able to draw a bead on them. They were safe—for the moment. Killian's mind ranged over the options a gunman would have. He could barge into the kitchen after her, or leave and wait back at her house. Or he could leave altogether and wait for another opportunity to kill Susannah.

Susannah shook her head violently and jabbed her finger repeatedly toward the door. She glanced up at Killian's hard, shadowy features. Her eyes widened even more when she spotted the pistol that he held with such casual ease. He was naked from the waist up, she realized, the moonlight accentuating his deep chest and his taut, leanly muscled body. Gulping, Susannah tore her attention back to the door, waiting to hear those heavy footsteps that had been pursuing her like hounds from hell. Her breathing was still harsh, but Killian's hand on her shoulder made her feel safer.

Killian looked around, his hearing keyed to any strange noises. Surprised that the Andersons hadn't awakened with the amount of noise Susannah had made, he glanced down at her. Undiminished panic still showed in her eyes. One hand was pressed against her heaving breast. She looked as if every nerve in her body were raw from whatever she'd just experienced.

Leaning down, he met and held her wide, searching gray eyes. "Susannah, what happened? Was someone after you?"

She nodded her head violently. Her mother always had a pencil and paper on the kitchen table for her. She grabbed them and hastily scrawled a message.

A man! A man tried to get in the window of my bedroom!

Killian's eyes narrowed.

Susannah gasped raggedly as she held his burning, intense gaze.

He patted her shoulder, hoping the gesture would offer her some sense of security. "You stay put, understand? I'm going to try and find him. I'll go back to your house and have a look around."

Susannah gave a low cry, and the meaning of the sound was clear as she gripped Killian's arm and shook her head. *No! No, don't go! He's out there! He'll kill you! Oh, please, don't go! He's after me, not you!*

Killian understood her silent plea for him to remain with her. But it was impossible under the circumstances. "Shh... I'll be all right," he said soothingly. "I want you to stay here. You'll be safer."

Gulping unsteadily, Susannah nodded, unwillingly releasing him.

With a look meant to give her solace, Killian rasped, "I'll be right back. I promise."

Shaking badly in the aftermath of her terrified run, Susannah sat huddled in the chair, feeling suddenly chilled in her damp cotton gown. Killian moved soundlessly, like a cougar, toward the door. But as he opened it and moved out into the night, Susannah felt a new wave of anguish and fear. Killian could be murdered!

* * *

Weaving in and around the fruit trees, the dew-laden grass soaking his bare feet and pajama legs, Killian quickly circled the Anderson house. If the killer was around, he wasn't here. Moving with the soundlessness of a shadow, he avoided the regular path and headed for Susannah's house. As he ran silently through the orchard, a slice of moon and the resulting silvery light allowed him to penetrate the night. Reaching the old homestead, his pistol held upward, Killian advanced toward the rear of the house, every sense screamingly alert. His nostrils flared, he inhaled, trying to get a whiff of any odor other than the sweet orchard fragrances.

Locating Susannah's bedroom at the rear, Killian saw nothing unusual. Remaining near a small grove of lilac bushes that were at least twenty feet tall, he waited. Patience was the name of the game. His original plan to remain at the Anderson house obviously wasn't a good one, he thought grimly as he waited. Frustration ate at him. He'd have to find a way to stay at Susannah's home in order to protect her. The chill of the predawn air surrounded him, but he was impervious to it.

His gaze scouted the surrounding area, his ears tuned in to pick up any sound. *Nothing.* Killian waited another ten minutes before moving toward the house. The killer could be inside, waiting for Susannah to return. His mouth dry, he compressed his lips into a thin line and quietly stole toward the homestead. His heart set up a sledgehammer pounding in his chest as he eased toward the open back door, the only entrance to the house. Wrapping both hands around the butt of his gun, Killian froze near the door frame. Susannah had left so quickly that the screen door was ajar, as well.

Still, there was no sound that was out of place. But Killian wasn't about to trust the potentially volatile situation. Moving quickly, he dived inside, his pistol aimed. Silence. His eyes mere slits, he remained crouched and tense as he passed through the gloomy kitchen, his head swiveling from side to side, missing nothing, absorbing everything. The living room was next. Nothing.

Finally, after ending the search in Susannah's bedroom, Killian checked the windows. Both were open to allow the fresh early-fall coolness to circulate. One window's screen was in place; the other screen, on the window behind her brass bed, was ripped and in need of repair. Going outside, Killian checked carefully for footprints around either of the bedroom windows, but the grass next to the house was tall and undisturbed. He noticed that as he walked distinct footprints appeared in the heavily dew-laden grass. There were no previous footprints to indicate the presence of an intruder.

Grimly Killian headed back toward the Anderson house, still staying away from the path, still alert, but convinced now that Susannah had experienced a nightmare about her assailant. Relief showered over him at the realization. Still, the incident had put him on notice not to allow the idyllic setting to relax him too much. Dawn was barely crawling onto the horizon, a pale lavender beneath the dark, retreating mantle of the night sky. A rooster was already crowing near the chicken coop as Killian stepped lightly onto the wooden porch.

Susannah met him at the screen door, her eyes huge with silent questions.

"There wasn't anyone," Killian told her as he entered the quiet kitchen. He noticed that Susannah had put a teakettle on the stove and lit the burner beneath it. He saw her eyes go wider with shock at his terse statement. Her gaze traveled to the pistol that was still in his hand, and he realized that it was upsetting her.

"Let me put this away and get decent. I'll be out in a moment. Your folks awake yet?"

Susannah shook her head. Despite her fear, she felt herself respond to the male beauty of Killian's tall, taut body. Black hair covered his chest in abundance, a dark strip trailing down across his flat, hard belly and disappearing beneath the drawstring of the pajamas that hung low on his hips. Susannah gulped, avoiding his narrowed, burning gaze.

In his bedroom, Killian quickly changed into jeans and a white short-sleeved shirt. He pulled on dark blue socks and slipped into a pair of comfortable brown loafers, then ran his fingers through his mussed hair, taming the short strands back into place. Then he strapped on his shoulder holster and slid the pistol into place.

Rubbing his hand across his stubbled jaw, Killian moved back to the kitchen, still amazed that the Andersons had slept through all the commotion. All the more reason, he warned himself, to stay alert for Susannah's sake.

When he entered the kitchen, he saw that she had poured him a cup of tea in a flowery china cup. She was sitting at the table, her hand gripping the note-pad and pencil, as if she had been waiting for his return. Killian sat down next to her.

"You had a nightmare," he told her. "That was all."

Susannah rapidly wrote a note on the pad and turned it around for Killian to read.

Impossible! I saw his shadow!

Killian picked up the tea and sipped it, enjoying the clean, minty taste. "There was no trace of footprints around either of your bedroom windows," he explained apologetically. "I searched your house carefully and found nothing. It was a dream, Susannah."

No! Susannah sat back, her arms folded across her breasts, and stared at his darkly etched features while he drank the tea. After a moment, she scribbled on the pad again.

I saw him! I saw the face of the man who nearly killed me!

Killian saw the bleak frustration, and fear in her gray eyes. Without thinking, he placed his hand over hers. "You remember what he looks like?" Before, she'd been unable to identify her assailant.

She nodded.

"Good. The police need an identification." Realizing he was gently cupping her cool hand, Killian pulled his back and quickly picked up his teacup. What the hell was going on? Couldn't he control his own actions? The idea frightened him. Susannah seemed unconsciously to bring out his softer side. But along with that softer side lurked the monstrous danger that could hurt her. He took a sip from the cup and set it down. His words came out clipped—almost angry.

"When you settle down over this, I want you to draw a picture of his face. I can take it to the police—it might give them a lead."

Hurt by his sudden gruffness, Susannah sat there, still taking in Killian's surprising words. *A nightmare?* How could it have been? It had been so *real!* Touching her forehead, which was now beginning to ache in earnest, Susannah closed her eyes and tried to get a grip on her rampant emotions. Killian's warm, unexpected touch had momentarily soothed her apprehension and settled her pounding heart—but just as quickly he'd withdrawn.

Opening her eyes, she wrote:

I'll draw a picture of him later, when I feel up to it.

Killian nodded, still edgy. One part of him was keyed to Susannah, the other to the door, the windows, and any errant sound. He knew his shoulder holster disturbed her. She kept glancing at him, then at the holster, a question in her eyes. How much could he tell her? How much *should* he tell her? He sensed her curiosity about him and his reasons for being here.

Feeling utterly trapped, Killian tried to think clearly. Being around Susannah seemed to scramble his emotions. He'd been too long without softness in his life. *And,* Killian lectured himself, *it would have to re-*

main that way. Still, he couldn't let go of the memory of the wonderful sensation of her pressed against him. He should have thrown her to the floor instead of using himself as a human shield to protect her, he thought in disgust. That way he wouldn't have had to touch her, to be reminded of all that he ached to have and never could. But he hadn't been thinking clearly; he'd reacted instinctively.

Grimly he held her gaze. "From now on, Susannah, you need to stay here, in your folks' home, where it's safer."

I will not stay here! I can't! If it was just a dream, then I'll be okay out there. I don't want to stay here.

He studied her in the silence, noting the set of her delicate jaw and the flash of stubbornness in her eyes. With a sigh, he set the cup down on the saucer.

"No. You'll stay here. In *this* house."

Susannah shook her head.

You don't understand! I tried to stay here when I got home from the hospital. I had awful dreams! If I stay in my room, I can't sleep. At the other house I feel safer. I don't have as many nightmares. I don't know why. I can't explain it, but I will not come and stay here.

Killian studied the scribbled note, utterly thwarted. No one knew better than he did about the night and the terrible dreams that could stalk it. He understood Susannah's pleading request, probably better than anyone else could. His heart squeezed at the pain in her admission, because he'd too long lived a similar life. With a sigh, he muttered, "All right, but then I'm staying at your place with you until we can get this settled. I need to know for sure whether this guy is real or just a dream."

Shocked, Susannah stared at him, her mouth dropping open. She felt the brutal hardness around him again and saw anger, touched with anxiety in his eyes. Her mind reeled with questions as the adrenaline left her bloodstream and left her shaky in its aftermath. With a trembling hand, she wrote:

Who are you? You carry a gun. I don't think you are who you say you are. Morgan suspects something, doesn't he? Please, tell me the truth, even if you don't tell my parents. I deserve to know.

Killian fingered the note, refusing to meet her challenging gaze. Stunned by Susannah's intuitive grasp of the situation, he realized he had to tell her. Otherwise, she'd never allow him to stay at her house.

"All right," he growled, "here's the truth. Morgan suspects that the man who tried to kill you will come and hunt you down once he knows you survived. You can ID him, and he's going to try to kill you before you can do it." He saw Susannah's eyes grow dark with shock. Angry that he had to hurt her with the truth, Killian snapped, "I'm here on assignment. I'm to protect you. Please don't tell your parents my real reason for being here. Morgan feels they've been through enough. I wasn't going to tell you, dammit, but you're so stubborn, you didn't leave me any recourse. I can't have you staying alone at the other house."

Susannah felt Killian's anger buffet her. Despite her fear and shock, she felt anger toward him even more.

How dare you! How dare Morgan! You should have told me this in the first place!

Killian didn't like being put in the middle, and he glared at her. "Look, I do as I'm ordered. I'm breaking my word in telling you this, and I'll probably catch hell from my boss for doing it. I don't like this any more than you do. If you want all of the truth, I don't even want to be here—I don't take assignments that involve women. But Morgan threatened to fire me if I didn't take this mission, so you and I are in the same boat. You don't want me here, and I damn well don't want to be here!"

Stunned, Susannah blinked at the powerful wave of feeling behind his harsh words. She sensed a desperation in Killian's anger, and it was that desperation that defused her own righteous anger.

I'm sorry, Killian. I shouldn't be angry with you.

He shook his head and refused to meet her eyes. The frightening truth was, every time he did, he wanted simply to find his way into her arms and be held. "Don't apologize," he muttered. "It isn't your fault, either. We're both caught between a rock and a hard place."

Without thinking, Susannah slowly raised her hand and placed it across Killian's clenched one on the table. His head snapped up as her fingers wrapped around his. The anger dissolved in his eyes, and for just a moment Susannah could have sworn she saw longing in his stormy gaze. But, just as quickly, it was gone, leaving only an icy coldness. She removed her hand from his, all too aware that he was rejecting her touch.

All she had wanted to do was comfort Killian. From her work, Susannah knew the healing nature of human touch firsthand. Killian had looked positively torn by the fact that he had to be here with her. Susannah had wanted to let him know somehow that she understood his dilemma. He didn't want anything to do with her because she was a woman. Her curiosity was piqued, but she knew better than to ask. Right now, Killian was edgy, turning the cup around and around in his long, spare hands.

You don't have to stay out there with me.

Killian made a muffled sound and stood up suddenly. He moved away from the table, automatically checking the window with his gaze. "Yes," he said irritably, "I do. I don't like it any more than you do, but it has to be done."

But it was a nightmare! You said so yourself. You can stay here with my folks.

Killian savagely spun on his heel, and when he spoke his voice was hoarse. "There's nothing you can say that will change my mind. You need protection, Susannah."

With a trembling hand, Susannah touched her brow. It was nerve-racking enough to stay by herself at the abandoned farmhouse. She was desperately afraid of the dark, of the terrors that came nightly when she lay down as her overactive imagination fueled the fires of her many fears. But Killian staying with her? He was so blatantly male—so quiet, yet so capable. Fighting her own feelings toward him, she sat for a good minute before writing on the notepad again.

Please tell my folks the truth about this. I don't want to lie to them about the reason you're staying out at the house with me. It would seem funny to them if you suddenly started living out there with me.

Killian couldn't disagree with her. He paced the room quietly, trying to come up with a better plan. He stopped and looked down at her exhausted features.

"I'll talk to them this morning."

Relief flowed through Susannah, and she nodded.

Morgan was trying to protect us, but this is one time when we should know the whole truth.

"I tried to tell him that," Killian said bitterly. He stood by the table, thinking. "That's all water under the bridge now," he said. "You saw the killer's face in your nightmare. I need you to draw a picture of him this morning so that I can take it to the police station. They'll fax it to Lexington and to Morgan."

Trying to combat the automatic reactions of fear, rage and humiliation that came with remembering, Susannah nodded. Her hand still pressed against her brow, she tried to control the cold-bladed anxiety triggered by the discussion.

It was impossible for Killian to steel himself against the clarity of the emotions he read in Susannah's pale face. "Easy," he said soothingly. "Take some deep breaths, Susannah, and the panic will start to go away." He watched her breasts rise and fall sharply beneath her wrinkled cotton gown, and he couldn't help thinking how pretty she looked in the thin garment with lace sewn around its oval neckline. She was like that lace, fragile and easily crushed, he realized as he stood watching her wrestle with her fear.

Miraculously, Susannah felt much of her panic dissolve beneath his husky-voiced instructions. She wasn't sure if it was because of the deep breaths or merely Killian's quiet presence. How did he know what she was experiencing? He must have experienced the very same thing, otherwise he wouldn't know how to help her. And he was helping her—even if he'd made it clear that he didn't want to be here.

"Good," Killian said gruffly as she became calm. He poured them more tea and took his chair again. "I'll sleep in the bedroom down the hall from yours. I'm a restless sleeper," he warned her sharply. "I have nightmares myself...." His voice trailed off.

Susannah stared at him, swayed by the sincerity in his dark blue eyes. There was such torment in them. Toward her? Toward the assignment? She just wasn't sure. Morning light was stealing through the ruffled curtains at the window now, softening his harsh features.

Nervously fingering the rectangular notepad, Susannah frowned, uncertain of her own feelings as she was every time he was with her.

"I won't bother you, if that's what you're worried about," he added when he saw the confusion on her face. He prayed he could keep his word—hoped against hope that he wouldn't have one of the terrible, wrenching nightmares that haunted him.

Agitated, Susannah got to her feet and moved to the window. The pale lavender of dawn reminded her of the color of her favorite flowers—the lilacs. Pressing and releasing her fingers against the porcelain sink, she thought about Killian's statement.

Killian studied Susannah in the quiet of the kitchen. Her dark hair lay mussed against her tense shoulders, a sable cloak against the pristine white of her nightgown. Killian ached to touch her hair, to tunnel his fingers through it and find out what it felt like. Would it be as soft as her body had been against his? Or more coarse, in keeping with the ramrod-straight spine that showed her courage despite the circumstances?

"Look," he said, breaking the tense silence, "maybe this will end sooner than I expect. I'll work on the house over there to stay close in case something happens. I'll paint and fix up the windows, the doors." *Anything to keep my mind off you.*

Turning, Susannah looked at him. He sat at the table, his long fingers wrapped around the dainty china cup on the yellow oilcloth. His body was hunched forward, and he had an unhappy expression on his face. She would never forget the look in his eyes, his alertness, or the sense of safety she'd felt when she'd fallen sobbing into his arms at the back door. Why was she hedging now about allowing him to be near her?

Licking her lips, she nodded. Suddenly more tired than she could remember ever being, she left the counter. It was time to go home. When she got to the screen door, Killian moved quickly out of his chair.

"I'll walk you back," Killian said, his tone brooking no argument. Opening the screen door, she walked out.

Although he wanted Susannah to believe he was relaxed, Killian remained on high alert as they trod the damp path through the orchard back to her home. The sky had turned a pale pink. It wouldn't be long before the sun came up.

Killian felt Susannah's worry as she looked around, her arms wrapped tightly around herself. He wanted to step close—to place a protective arm around her shoulders and give her the sense of security she so desperately needed and so richly deserved. Yet he knew that touching her would melt his defenses. That couldn't happen—ever. Killian swore never to allow Susannah to reach inside him; but she had that ability, and he knew it. Somehow, he had to strengthen his resolve and keep her at arm's length. At all costs. For her own sake.

"Maybe if I patch that torn screen in your bedroom and put some locks on the windows, you'll feel better about being there." He saw her flash him a grateful look. "I'll tell your folks what happened when they get up. Then I'll contact Morgan."

Susannah nodded her agreement. She longed simply to step closer to Killian, to be in his protective embrace again. She couldn't forget the lean power of his body against hers, the way he'd used himself as a barrier to protect her.

She wrestled with conflicting feelings. Why was Killian so unhappy about having to stay out at the house with her? She couldn't help how she felt. She knew that right now, if she went back to her old room at her folks' house, the nightmares would return. Her life had begun to stabilize—until tonight. If only Killian could understand why she had to be at the old homestead.

"I'll make sure your house is safe. Then I want you to get some sleep. When you get up, you can draw me the face you saw in the nightmare."

Killian saw Susannah's eyes darken.

"Don't worry, I'll be around. You may not know it, but I'll be there. Like a shadow."

Shivering, Susannah nodded. Her life had turned into nothing but a series of shadows. Killian's body against hers had been real, and never had she needed that more. But Killian didn't like her, didn't want to be with her. She swallowed her need to be held, still grateful that Killian would be nearby. Perhaps her mind was finally ready to give up the information it had seen, and that should help in the long run.

Touching her throat, she fervently wished her voice would come back. At least now she could make some noise, and that seemed a hopeful sign. She stole a glance up into Killian's grim, alert features. She'd welcome his company, even though he didn't want hers. Right now, she needed the human contàct. Thinking back, she realized that the anger she'd sensed in Killian had been due to his not wanting to take the assignment. It hadn't really been aimed directly at her. Sometimes it was lonely out there at the homestead. He wasn't a willing guest, Susannah reminded herself. Still, if her attacker was really out there, she would feel a measure of safety knowing that Killian was nearby.

After thoroughly checking Susannah's home again, Killian allowed her into the farmhouse. He'd double-check around the house and quietly search the acreage around it just to make sure no one was hiding in wait. At the bedroom door, Susannah shyly turned and gave him a soft, hesitant smile. A thank-you showed clearly in her eyes, and it took everything Killian had for him to turn away from her. "I'll be over about noon," he rasped, more gruffly than he'd intended.

Susannah waited for Killian's promised noon arrival as she sat at her kitchen table. She questioned herself. Her real home was in town, near the school where she taught. Why didn't she have the courage to move back there? Glumly she admitted it was because she was afraid of being completely alone. At least this broken-down homestead was close to her parents.

Killian deliberately made noise as he stepped up on Susannah's porch, carrying art supplies under one arm. He knew all about being jumpy. He'd decked more than one man who had inadvertently come up behind him without warning. Wolf had been one of those men, on assignment down in Peru. The others on the team had learned from his mistake and had always let Killian know they were coming.

Susannah was waiting for him at the screen door. She looked beautiful, clothed in a long, lightweight denim skirt and a fuchsia short-sleeved blouse. She'd tied her hair back with a pink ribbon, and soft tendrils brushed her temples. Killian tensed himself against the tempting sight of her.

Stepping into the kitchen, Killian sniffed. "You've got coffee on?" He found himself wanting to ease the seriousness out of her wary eyes. The dark shadows beneath them told him she hadn't slept well since the nightmare.

Placing sketch pad, colored pencils and eraser on the table, Killian eased into a chair. Susannah went to the cupboard, retrieved a white ceramic mug and poured him some coffee. He nodded his thanks as she came over and handed it to him.

"Sit down," he urged her. "We've got some work to do."

Looking over the art supplies, Susannah sat down at his elbow. Somehow Killian looked heart-stoppingly handsome and dangerous all at once. His dress was casual, but she always sensed the inner tension in him, and could see some undefinable emotion in his blue eyes when he looked at her. But the anger was no longer there, she noted with relief.

"I'd like you to sketch for me the man you saw in your nightmare," Killian said.

Hesitant, Susannah fingered the box of colored pencils. Her throat constricted, and she closed her eyes for a moment. How could she make Killian understand that since the attack her love of drawing and painting had gone away?

"It doesn't have to be fancy, Susannah. Draw me something. Anything. I have a way to check what you sketch for me against police mug shots." He saw pain in her eyes, and her lower lip trembled as she withdrew her hand from the box of pencils. He cocked his head. "What is it?" He recalled his sister's pain, and the hours he'd spent holding her while she cried after realizing her once-beautiful face was gone forever. A powerful urge to reach out and give Susannah that same kind of help nearly overwhelmed him, but he reared back inwardly. He couldn't.

With a helpless shrug, Susannah swallowed against the lump and shakily opened up the sketch pad. She had to try. She believed in Killian, and she believed he could help her. Suddenly embarrassed, she took her pad and pencil and wrote:

I'm rusty at this. I haven't drawn since being wounded.

He grimaced. "I'm no art critic, Susannah. I can't draw a straight line. Anything you can do will look great to me. Give it your best try."

Susannah picked up a pencil and began to sketch. She tried to concentrate on the task at hand, but she found her senses revolving back to Killian's overwhelming presence. All morning she'd thought about him staying here with her. It wasn't him she couldn't trust, she realized—it was herself! The discovery left her feeling shaken. Never had a man influenced her on all levels, as Killian did. What was it about him? For the thousandth time, Susannah ached to have her voice back. If only she could talk!

Quiet descended upon them. Killian gazed around the kitchen, keenly aware of Susannah's presence. It was like a rainbow in his dismal life. There were at least forty colorful drawings tacked to the kitchen walls, obviously done by very young children. Probably her class. Peace, a feeling that didn't come often to Killian, descended gently around him. Was it the old-fashioned house? Being out in the country away from the madding crowd? Or—he swung his gaze back to Susannah and saw her brows drawn together in total concentration, her mouth pursed—was it her?

Unconsciously Killian's shoulders dropped, and he eased the chair back off its two front legs, loosely holding the mug of coffee against his belly. Birds, mostly robins, were singing and calling to one another. The sweet scents of grass, ripening fruit and clean mountain air wafted through the kitchen window. Susannah had a small radio on in the corner, and FM music flowed softly across the room, like an invisible caress.

His gaze settled on Susannah's ponytail, and he noted the gold and red glints between the sable strands. Her hair was thick and luxurious. A man could drive himself crazy wondering what the texture of it was like, Killian decided unhappily. Right now, he knew his focus had to be on keeping her protected, not his own personal longings.

The sketch of the man took shape beneath Susannah's slender fingers over the next hour. Frequently she struggled, erasing and beginning again. Killian marveled at her skill as an artist. She might consider herself rusty, but she was definitely a professional.

Finally her mouth quirked and she glanced up. Slowly she turned the sketch toward him.

"Unsavory-looking bastard," Killian whispered as he put the coffee aside and held the sketch up to examine it. "Brown eyes, blond hair and crooked front teeth?"

Susannah nodded. She saw the change in Killian's assessing blue eyes. A fierce anger emanated from him, and she sensed his hatred of her attacker.

He reminds me of a weasel, with close-set eyes that are small and beady-looking.

Killian nodded and put the sketch aside. "I'll take this to the police department today. I called Morgan. He knows you've remembered what your attacker looked like, so he's anxious to get this, too. He'll know what to do with it. If this bastard has a police record, we'll be on the way to catching him."

Chilled, Susannah slowly rubbed her arms with her hands.

Killian felt her raw fear. But he stopped himself from reaching out to give her a touch of reassurance. Gathering up the sketch, he rose. "I'll be back as soon as I can. In the meantime, you stay alert."

The warning made another chill move through her as she looked up at him. Somehow, some of the tension around him was gone. The peace that naturally inhabited the farmhouse had always worked wonders on her own nervousness, and Susannah realized that it might be doing the same for him. She nodded in agreement to his orders.

caress

He'd give his life for her, if necessary, he realized suddenly. Susannah was worth dying for.

if you went down
gone. They know the
atchful for you. In the

disagree with him. The
guard and watchful, the
nding her. Rising, she left

d her as they walked across th
ll be over soon.''
nah's eyes sparkled with such
ith gratitude, that Killian had
from reaching out to

Chapter Four

Susannah was helping her mother can ripe figs in the kitchen when she saw Killian return from Glen. She stood at the counter and watched him emerge from the four-wheel-drive Land Cruiser. The vehicle seeming fitting for a man like Killian, she thought, a man who was rugged, a loner, iconoclastic. Though his face remained emotionless, his roving blue gaze held her, made her feel an inherent safety as he looked around the property. Her heart took a skipping beat as he turned and headed into the house.

"Killian's home," Pansy said. She shook her head as she transferred the recently boiled figs to the jars awaiting on the counter. "I'm so nervous now." With a little laugh, she noted, "My hands haven't stopped shaking since he told us the truth this morning."

Wanting somehow to reassure her, Susannah put her arms around her mother and gave her a hug.

Killian walked into the kitchen and saw Susannah embracing her mother. He halted, a strange, twisting feeling moving through him. Mother and daughter held each other, and he remained motionless. It was Susannah who sensed his presence first. She loosened the hug and smiled shyly in his direction.

Pansy tittered nervously when she realized he was standing in the doorway. "I didn't hear you come in, Mr. Killian."

"I should have said something," he said abruptly. Killian felt bad for the woman. Ever since he'd told the Andersons the truth, it had been as if a shock wave had struck the farm. Sam Anderson had promptly gone out to the barn to fix a piece of machinery. Pansy had suddenly gotten busy with canning duties. Staying occupied was one way to deal with tension, Killian realized. His gaze moved to Susannah, whose cheeks were flushed. Her hair was still in a ponytail, the tendrils sticking to her dampened temples with the heat of the day and the lack of breeze through the kitchen. She looked beautiful.

"Did you tell the police?" Pansy asked, nervously wiping her hands on her checked apron.

"Yes. Everyone has a copy of the picture Susannah sketched. Morgan will call me here if they find out who it is. The FBI's in on it, so maybe we'll turn up something a little sooner."

Susannah heard her mother give a little moan, and she reached over and touched her shoulder and gave her a look she hoped she could decipher.

"Oh, I'm okay, honey," Pansy said in response, patting her hand in a consoling way.

Killian absorbed the soft look Susannah gave her worried mother. She had such sensitivity. How he wished he could have that in his life. A sadness moved through him, and he turned away, unable to stand the compassion on Susannah's features.

"Is Sam still out at the barn?" he demanded.

"Yes."

"I'll go help him," Killian said, and left without another word.

An odd ache had filled Susannah as she watched Killian's carefully arranged face give way to his real feelings. There had been such naked hunger in his eyes that it left her feeling in touch with herself as a woman as never before. She tried to help her mother, unable to get Killian's expression out of her mind—or her heart.

"That Mr. Killian's a strange one," Pansy said, to no one in particular, as she spooned the figs into a jar, their fragrant steam rising around her. "He's so gruff. Almost rude. But he cares. I can feel it around him. I wonder why he's so standoffish? It's hard to get close to him, to let him know how grateful we are for him being here."

Susannah nodded. Killian *was* gruff—like a cranky old bear. It was part of what he used to keep people at bay, she thought. Yet, just a few minutes ago, she'd seen the real Sean Killian—a man who had wants—and desires. And her heart wouldn't settle down over that discovery.

Around four o'clock, Pansy sent Susannah out with a gallon of iced tea and two glasses for the men, who were still laboring in the barn. The sunlight was bright and hot for an early-September day, and Susannah reveled in it. Chickens scattered out of her path as she crossed the dirt driveway to the barn, which sat off to one side of the green-and-white farmhouse.

As she entered the huge, airy structure, the familiar smell of hay and straw filled her nostrils. At one end of the barn, where the machinery was kept, Susannah spotted her father working intently on his tractor. The engine had been pulled up and out of the tractor itself and hung suspended by two chains looped around one of the barn's huge upper beams. She saw Killian down on his knees, working beneath the engine while her father stood above him. They were trying to thread a hose from above the engine to somewhere down below, where Killian leaned beneath it, his hand outstretched for it.

Killian had clearly shed his shirt long before, and his skin glistened with sweat from the hot barn air, accentuating his muscular chest and arms. A lock of black hair stuck damply to his forehead as he frowned in concentration, intent on capturing the errant hose.

Susannah slowed her step halfway to them. Her father turned away from the tractor, going to the drawer where he kept many of his tools. Just then, she heard a vague snap. Her eyes rose to the beam that held the heavy engine. Instantly her gaze shifted to Killian, who seemed oblivious of the sound, his concentration centered on threading the hose through the engine.

Sam Anderson was still bent over a drawer, rummaging for a tool.

Susannah realized that the chain was slowly coming undone. At any second it would snap free and that heavy tractor engine would fall on Killian! Without thinking, she cried out a warning. *"Look out, Killian!"*

Her scream shattered the barn's musty stillness.

Killian jerked his hand back and heard a cracking, metallic sound. He glanced to his left and saw Susannah, her finger pointing toward the beam above him. Sam had whirled around at the cry. In one motion, Killian leaped away from the engine.

Susannah clutched the jar of iced tea to her as she saw the chain give way. She screamed as the tractor engine slammed heavily down on the barn floor. But Killian was leaping away as the engine fell, rolling through the straw and dust on the floor.

Setting the iced tea aside, Susannah ran toward him, unsure whether he was hurt or not. He lay on his side, his back to her, as she raced up to him.

"Killian?" she sobbed. "Killian? Are you hurt?" She fell to her knees, reaching out to touch him.

"Good God!" Sam Anderson hurried to Killian's side. "Son? You all right?"

Breathing raggedly, Susannah touched Killian's hard, damp shoulder. He rolled over onto his back, his eyes narrowed and intense.

"Are—are you all right?" she stammered, quickly glancing down his body, checking for blood or a sign of injury.

"I'm fine," Killian rasped, sitting up. Then he grew very still. He saw the look in Susannah's huge eyes, saw her expressive fingers resting against her swan-like throat. Her face was pale. He blinked. Susannah had spoken. Her eyes still mirrored her fear for him, and he felt the coolness of her fingers resting on his dirty arm.

"You're sure?" Susannah demanded breathlessly, trading a look with her father, who knelt on the other side of Killian. "You could have been killed!" Badly shaken, she stared down into his taut face and held his burning gaze. Killian was like a lean, bronzed statue, his gleaming muscles taut from the hard physical labor.

Sam gasped and stared at his daughter. "Honey, you're talking!"

Gasping herself, Susannah reared back on her heels, her hands flying to her mouth. She saw Killian grin slightly. It was true! She had spoken! With a little cry, Susannah touched her throat, almost unbelieving. "Pa, I got my voice back...."

Killian felt Susannah's joy radiating from her like sunlight itself. He felt embraced and lifted by her joy at her discovery. And what a beautiful voice she had— low and husky. A tremor of warning fled through him as he drowned in her shining eyes. This was just one more thing to like about Susannah, to want from her.

Susannah's gaze moved from her father to Killian and back again. "I can speak! I can talk again!" Susannah choked, and tears streamed down her cheeks.

"Oh," Sam whispered unsteadily, "that's wonderful, honey!" He got to his feet and came around to where his daughter knelt. Leaning over, he helped her stand, then threw his arms around her and held her tight for a long, long time.

Touched, Killian remained quietly on the floor. The closeness of Sam with his daughter brought back good, poignant memories of his early home life, of his mother's strength and love. Slowly he eased himself to his feet and began to brush off the straw that clung to his damp skin. Sam and Susannah were laughing and crying, their brows touching. Tears jammed unexpectedly into Killian's eyes, and he quickly blinked them away. What the hell was happening to him?

Turning away from the happy scene, Killian went to retrieve his shirt. Disgruntled and shaken at his own emotional response, he tried to avoid looking at Susannah. It was *her*. Whatever magic it was that she wielded as a woman, it had a decided effect on him, whether he wanted it to or not. Agitated, Killian buttoned his shirt, stuffed the tail into his jeans and gathered up the broken chain, which lay across the floor and around the engine.

"Come on, honey, let's go tell Ma," Sam quavered, his arm around his daughter's shoulders. He gave Killian a grateful look. "You, too. You deserve to be a part of the celebration."

Killian shrugged. "No... you folks go ahead...."

Susannah eased out of her father's embrace and slowly approached Killian. How beautifully and dangerously male he was. Her senses were heightened to almost a painful degree, giving her an excruciating awareness of his smoldering, hooded look as she approached. His chiseled mouth was drawn in at the corners.

"You're okay?" Susannah breathed softly. Then she stepped back, blushing.

Shocked by her unexpected concern for him despite what had happened to her, Killian was at a loss for words. He gripped the chain in his hands. "I'm okay," he managed in a strangled tone. "Go share the news with your mother...." he ordered unsteadily. What a beautiful voice she had, Killian thought dazedly, reeling from the feelings her voice stirred within him.

Trapped beneath his sensual, scorching gaze, Susannah's lips parted. What would it be like to explore that mouth endlessly, that wonderful mouth that was now pursed into a dangerous, thin line of warning? Every nerve in her body responded to his look of hunger. It was the kind of look that made Susannah wildly aware that she was a woman, in all ways. It was not an insulting look, it was a look of desire—for her alone.

"Come on, honey," Sam said happily as he came up and patted her shoulder, "let's go share the good news with Ma. She's gonna cry a bucket of tears over this."

Killian remained still, nearly overwhelmed by his need to reach out and touch Susannah's mussed hair or caress her flushed cheek. He watched as father and daughter left the barn together. Their happiness surrounded him like a long-lost memory. Taking a deep, steadying breath, Killian began to unhook the ends of the chain from the engine. His mind was waging war with his clamoring heart and his aching body. Susannah could now tell them what had happened to her. His emotions were in utter disarray. Her voice was soft and husky, like a well-aged Irish whiskey.

Angrily Killian cleaned up the mess in the barn and put the chains aside. In a way, he felt chained to the situation at the farm, he thought—chained to Susannah in a connection he could neither fight nor flee. Never had a woman gotten to him as Susannah had. His relationships with women had been few and brief—one-night stands that allowed him to leave before darkness came and made an enemy out of anyone who dared get close to him. What was it about Susannah that was different? The need to explore her drove him out of the barn. He slowly walked toward the farmhouse, savagely jamming down his fiery needs. Maybe now he could talk to Susannah about the assault, he reasoned.

Pansy was serving up lemonade in tall purple glasses in celebration. Susannah felt Killian's approach at the screen door before he appeared. What was this synchronicity the two of them seemed to share? Puzzled, but far too joyous over her voice returning to spend time worrying, she gave him a brilliant, welcoming smile as he walked into the kitchen.

"Sit down, son," Sam thundered. "You've earned yourself a glass of Ma's special hand-squeezed lemonade."

Killian hesitated. He'd hoped to come into the house, go to his room, take a cold shower and settle his roiling emotions. But the looks on their faces made him decide differently. With a curt nod, he took a seat opposite Susannah. Her eyes sparkled like diamonds caught in sunlight. He felt himself becoming helplessly ensnared in the joy that radiated around her like a rainbow of colors.

Pansy gave him the lemonade, gratitude visible in every line of her worn face.

"Killian, we're glad you're all right," she said. "Thank goodness you weren't hurt." She reached over and patted Susannah's hand warmly. "Just hearin' Susannah's voice again is like hearin' the angels speakin'."

Killian sipped the icy lemonade, hotly aware of the fire within him, captive to Susannah's thankful gaze. "Your daughter saved me from a few broken bones," he muttered.

Sam hooted and said, "A few? Son, you would've had your back broken if my Susannah hadn't found her voice in time."

Killian nodded and stared down at the glass. If there was such a thing as an angelic woman, it was Susannah. Her skin glowed with renewed color, and her lips were stretched into a happy curve as she gripped her father's leathery brown hand. Killian absorbed the love and warmth among the family members. Nothing could be stronger or better than that, in his opinion. Except maybe the fevered love of a man who loved his woman with a blind passion that overrode the fear of death in him.

"I can't believe it! This is like a dream—I can talk again!" Susannah told him, her hand automatically moving to her throat.

Killian ruminated over the events. He was perfectly at ease with saving other people's lives—but no one, with the exception of his teammates in Peru, had ever saved him from certain death. And he had to admit to himself that Sam was correct: If not for Susannah he'd have a broken back at best—and at worst, he'd be dead. Killian was unsure how to feel about having a woman save his worthless hide. He had a blinding loyalty to those he fought beside, to those who saved him. He lifted his head and stared at Susannah. Things had changed subtly but irrevocably because of this event. No longer was Morgan's edict that he stay here and protect her hanging over his head like a threat.

Moving his fingers across the beaded coolness of the glass, Killian pondered the web of circumstances tightening around him. Perhaps his sense of honor was skewed. On one hand, Susannah deserved his best efforts to protect her. On the other hand, he saw himself as a danger to her each night he stayed at her home. What was he going to do? He could no longer treat her as a mere assignment—an object to be protected. Not that he'd been particularly successful with that tack before.

"Getting your voice back is going to be a big help," Killian offered lamely.

With a slight laugh, Susannah said, "I don't know if you'll feel that way or not, Sean. Pa says I talk too much." Susannah felt heat rise in her neck and into her face when his head snapped up, his eyes pinning her. She suddenly realized she'd slipped and used his first name. Vividly recalling that Killian had said that only his mother and sister used his first name, she groped for an apology. "I'm sorry, I forgot—you like to be called by your last name."

Killian shrugged, not wanting to make a big deal out of it. "You saved my life. I think that gives you the right to call me anything you want." His heart contracted at her husky, quavering words, and he retreated into silence, feeling that words were useless. Her voice, calling him Sean, had released a Pandora's box of deeply held emotions from his dark, haunted past. When she'd said his name, it had come out like a prayer. A beautiful, clean prayer of thanks. How little in his world was clean or beautiful. But somehow this woman giving him her lustrous look made him feel as if he were both. His head argued differently, but for once Killian ignored it.

With a happy smile, Pansy came over and rested her hands on her daughter's shoulders. "You two young'ns will stay for dinner, won't you? We have to celebrate!"

Killian wanted the safety of isolation. He shook his head. "I've got things to do, Mrs. Anderson." When he saw the regret in the woman's face, he got to his feet. He felt Susannah's eyes on him, as if she knew what he was doing and why he was doing it. "Thanks anyway," he mumbled, and quickly left the kitchen. His job was to protect this family, not to join it. Killian was relieved to escape, not sure how long he could continue to hold his emotions in check. As he stalked through the living room and down the hall to his bedroom, all he wanted was a cold shower to shock him back to the harsh reality he'd lived with since leaving Ireland so many years before. And somehow, he was going to have to dredge up enough control to be able to sleep under the same roof with Susannah. Somehow...

Early-evening light shed a subdued glow around the kitchen of Susannah's small house. Killian sat at the kitchen table and watched as she made coffee at the counter. He had insisted he wasn't hungry, but Pansy had sent a plate of food with him when he'd escorted Susannah back to her homestead. The meal had been simple but filling. Tonight he was more tense than he could recall ever being. He felt as if his emotions were caught in a desperate tug-of-war.

Was it because of Susannah's whiskey laughter, that husky resonance that made him feel as if she were reaching out and caressing him? Killian sourly tried to ignore what her breathy voice did to him.

"You sure ate your share of Ma's cherry pie, Sean," she said with a teasing look over her shoulder. Killian sat at the table, his chin resting forward on his chest, his chair tipped back on its rear legs. His narrow face was dark and thoughtful.

"It was good."

Chortling, Susannah retrieved the lovely flowered china cups and saucers from the oak cabinet. "You ate like a man who hasn't had too many home-cooked meals in his life."

Killian grudgingly looked at her as she came over and set the cups and saucers on the oilcloth. Her insight, as always, was unsettling to him. "I haven't," he admitted slowly.

Susannah hesitated. There was so much she wanted to say to him. She slid her fingers across the back of the wooden chair opposite him. "Sean, I need to talk to you. I mean really talk to you." Heat rushed up her neck and into her cheeks, and Susannah groaned, touching her flushed face. "I wish I didn't turn beet red all the time!"

Killian absorbed her discomfort. "In Ireland we'd call you a primrose—a woman with moonlight skin and red primroses for cheeks," he said quietly.

The utter beauty of his whispered words made Susannah stand in shocked silence. "You're a poet."

Uncomfortable, he muttered, "I don't think of myself in those terms."

She saw the wariness in his eyes and sensed that her boldness was making him edgy. "Is it a crime to say that a man possesses a soul that can see the world in terms of beauty?"

Relieved that Susannah had turned and walked back to the counter, Killian frowned. He studied her as he tried to formulate an answer to her probing question. Each movement of her hands was graceful—and each time she touched something, he felt as if she were touching him instead. Shaking his head, he wondered what the hell had gotten into him. He was acting like a man who'd been without a woman far too long. Well, hadn't he?

Clearing his throat, Killian said, "I'd rather talk about you than myself."

Susannah sat down, drying her hands on a green-and-white checked towel. "I know you would, but I'm not going to let you." She kept her voice light, because she sensed that if she pushed him too hard he'd close up. She opened her hands to him. "I need to clear the air on some things between us."

Killian's stomach knotted painfully. The fragrant smell of coffee filled the kitchen. "Go on," he said in a warning growl.

Susannah nervously touched her brow. "I'm actually afraid to talk to you. Maybe it's because of what happened, getting shot by that man. I don't know..."

"The hurt part, the wounded side of you, feels that fear," Killian told her, his tone less gruff now. "It was a man who nearly killed you. Why shouldn't you be afraid of men in general?" He had to stop himself from reaching out to touch her tightly clasped hands on the tabletop. Her knuckles were white.

"You seem to know so much about me—about what I'm feeling." She gave him a long, scrutinizing look. "How?"

Shifting uncomfortably, Killian shrugged. "Experience, maybe."

"Whose? Your own?" After all, he was a mercenary, Susannah reminded herself. A world-traveled and world-weary man who had placed his life on the line time and again.

"No... not exactly... My sister, Meg, was—" His mouth quirked at the corners. "She was beautiful, and had a promising career as a stage actress. Meg met and fell in love with an Irish-American guy, and they were planning on getting married." He cleared his throat and forced himself to finish. "She flew back to Ireland to be in a play—and at her stopover at Heathrow Airport a terrorist bomb went off."

"Oh, no..." Susannah whispered. "Is she...alive?"

The horror of that day came rushing back to Killian, and he closed his eyes, his voice low with feeling. "Yes, she's alive. But the bomb... She's badly disfigured. She's no longer beautiful. Her career ended, and I've seen her through fifteen operations to restore her face." Killian shrugged hopelessly. "Meg cut off her engagement to Ian, too, even though he wanted to stay with her. She couldn't believe that any man could love her like that."

"How awful," Susannah whispered. Reaching out, she slid her hand across his tightly clenched fist. "It must have been hard on you, too."

Wildly aware of Susannah's touch, Killian warned himself that she'd done it only out of compassion. Her fingers were cool and soft against his sun-toughened skin. His mouth went dry, and his heart rate skyrocketed. Torn between emotions from the past and the boiling heat scalding up through him, Killian rasped, "Meg has been a shadow of herself since then. She's fearful, always looking over her shoulder, has terrible nightmares, and doesn't trust anyone." Bitterly he added, "She's even wary of me, her own brother." It hurt to admit that, but Killian sensed that Susannah had the emotional strength to deal with his first-time admission to anyone about his sister.

Tightening her hand around his, Susannah ached for Killian. She saw the hurt and confusion in his eyes. "Everyone suffers when someone is hurt like that." Forcing herself to release Killian's hand, Susannah whispered, "Look what I've put my parents through since I awakened from the coma. Look how I distrusted you at first."

He gave her a hooded look. "You're better off if you do."

"No," Susannah said fervently, her voice quavering with feeling. "I don't believe that anymore, Sean. You put on a tough act, and I'm sure you're very tough emotionally, but I can read your eyes. I can see the trauma that Meg went through, and how it has affected you." She smiled slightly. "I may come from hill folk, but I've got two good eyes in my head, and a heart that's never led me wrong."

Killian struggled with himself. He'd never spoken to anyone about his sister—not even to Morgan. And now he was spilling his guts to Susannah. He said nothing, for fear of divulging even more.

"I'm really sorry about your sister. Is she living in America?"

"No. She lives near the Irish Sea, in a thatched hut that used to belong to a fisherman and his wife. They died and left her the place. Old Dun and his wife Em were like grandparents to Meg. They took care of her when I had to be on assignment. Meg can't stand being around people."

"It's hard for most people to understand how it feels to be a victim of violence," Susannah mused. She looked over at the coffeepot. The coffee was ready to be served. Rising, she added, "I know that since I woke up from the coma I've been jumpy and paranoid. If someone comes up behind me, I scream. If I catch sight of my own shadow unexpectedly I break out in a sweat and my heart starts hammering." She poured coffee into the cups. "Stupid, isn't it?"

Putting a teaspoon of sugar into the dark, fragrant coffee, Killian shook his head. "Not at all. I call it a survival reflex."

Coming back to the table and sitting down, Susannah gave him a weak smile. "Even now, I dread talking about what happened to me." She turned her hands over. "My palms are damp, and my heart is running like a rabbit's."

"Adrenaline," Killian explained gently, "the flight-or-fight hormone." He stirred the coffee slowly with the spoon, holding her searching gaze.

"Morgan only gave me a brief overview of what happened to you," he probed gently. "Why don't you fill me in on your version? It might help me do my job better."

Susannah squirmed. "This is really going to sound stupid, Sean. It was my idea to go visit Morgan and Laura." She looked around the old farmhouse. "I've never gone much of anywhere, except to Lexington to get my teaching degree. A lot of my friends teased me that I wasn't very worldly and all that. After graduating and coming back here, I bought myself a small house in Glen, near where I work at the local grade school. Laura had been begging me to come for a visit, and I thought taking a plane to Washington, D.C., would expand my horizons.''

Killian nodded. In many ways, Susannah's country ways had served to protect her from the world at large. Kentucky was a mountainous state with a small population, in some ways insulated from the harsher realities that plague big cities. ''Your first flight?''

She smiled. ''Yes, my first. It was really exciting.'' With an embarrassed laugh, she added, ''I know, where else would you find someone who hasn't flown on a plane in this day and age. I had such a wonderful time with Laura, with her children. Morgan took me to the Smithsonian Institution for the whole day, and I was in heaven. I love learning, and that is the most wonderful museum I've ever seen. On my way home I landed at Lexington and was on my way to the bus station to get back here to Glen.'' Her smile faded. ''That's when all this happened.''

''Were you in the bus station itself?''

Susannah shook her head. ''No. I'd just stepped off the bus. There was a row of ten buses parked under this huge roof, and my bus was farthest away from the building. I was the last one off the bus. It was very dark that night, and it was raining. A thunderstorm. The rain was whipping in under the roof, and I had my head down and was hurrying to get inside.

"This man came out of nowhere and began talking real fast to me. At the same time, he was reaching for my shoulder bag and pulling it off my arm. He was smiling and saying he'd like to help me."

"Was he acting nervous?" Killian asked, noticing that Susannah had gone pale recounting the event.

"I didn't realize it at the time, but yes, he was. How did you know that?"

"Because no doubt he spotted you as a patsy, someone gullible enough to approach, lie to, and then use your luggage—probably to hide drugs or money for a later pickup. But go on. What happened next?" Killian leaned forward, his hands around the hot mug of coffee.

Susannah took in a ragged breath. She was amazed by Killian's knowledge. She was so naive, and it had nearly gotten her killed. "He said he'd take my bag into the station for me. I didn't know what to do. He seemed so nice—he was smiling all the time. I was getting wet from the rain, and I was wearing a new outfit I'd bought, and I didn't want it ruined, so I let him have the bag." She flushed and looked down. "You know the worst part?" she whispered. "I was flattered. I thought he was interested in me...." Her voice trailed off.

Susannah rubbed her brow and was silent for a long moment. When she spoke again, her voice came out hoarse. "He'd no sooner put the piece of luggage over his shoulder than I saw this other man step out of the dark and shoot at him. I screamed, but it was too late. The man fell, and I saw the killer move toward me. No one else was around. No one else saw it happen." Susannah shuddered and wrapped her arms around herself. "The next thing I knew, the killer was after me. I ran into a nearby alley. I remember thinking I was going to die. I heard shots—I heard bullets hitting the sides of the building and whining around me."

Closing her eyes, she whispered, "I was running hard, choking for air. I slipped on the wet street, and it was so dark, so dark..." Susannah opened her eyes. "I remember thinking I had to try to scream for help. But no one came. The next thing I knew, something hit me in the head—a hot sensation. That's it."

Glancing over at Killian, Susannah saw anger flash in his narrowed eyes. Her voice went off-key. "I woke up two months later. My ma was at my side when I came around, and I remember her crying."

"It was probably a drug deal gone wrong," Killian growled. He stared down at his hands. He'd like to wrap them around that bastard and give him back what he'd done to Susannah. "You were at the wrong place at the wrong time. There may have been drugs left in a nearby locker that the man who talked to you was supposed to pick up. Or the guy may have been on the run, using you as a decoy, hoping the killer wouldn't spot him if he was part of a couple." He looked at her sadly. "I'm sorry it happened, Susannah."

"At least I'm alive. I survived." She shrugged, embarrassed. "So much for my trying to become more worldly. I was so stupid."

"No," Killian rasped, "not stupid. Just not as alert as you might have been."

Shivering, Susannah slowly rubbed her arms with her hands. "Sean...the other night when I woke up?"

"Yes?"

"Please believe me. There *was* a man outside my bedroom window. I heard him. I saw his shadow against the opposite wall of my bedroom."

With a sigh, Killian shook his head. "There was no evidence—no footprints outside either window, Susannah. The grass wasn't disturbed."

Rubbing her head with her hands, Susannah sat there, confused. "I could have sworn he was there."

Killian wanted to reach out and comfort her, but he knew he didn't dare. Just her sharing the tragedy with him had drawn her uncomfortably close to him. "Let me do the worrying about it," he said. "All I need you to do is continue to get well."

Susannah felt latent power swirling around him as he sat tautly at the table. Anger shone in his eyes, but this time she knew it wasn't aimed at her; it was aimed at her unidentified assailant.

"I never thought about the killer coming to finish me off," she told him lamely. "That's stupid, too."

"Naive."

"Whatever you want to call it, it still can get me killed." She gave him a long look. "Would this man kill my parents, too?"

"I don't know," Killian said, trying to soothe her worry. "Most of these men go strictly for the target. In a way, you're protecting your parents by not being in their house right now."

"But if the killer got my address, he might think I was at my home in Glen, right?"

"That would be the first place he'd look," Killian agreed, impressed with her insight.

"And then he'd do what?"

"Probably discreetly try to nose around some of your neighbors and find out where you are," he guessed.

"It's no secret I'm here," Susannah said unhappily. "And if the killer didn't know I was out here at the homestead, he might break into my folks' home to find me."

"Usually," he told her, trying to assuage her growing fear, "a contract killer will do a good deal of research to locate his target. That means he probably will show up here sooner or later. My hunch is that he'll stake out the place, sit with a field scope on a rifle, or a pair of binoculars, and try to figure out the comings and goings of everyone here. Once he knew for sure where you were and when to get you alone, he'd come for you."

A chill ran up her spine, and she stared over at Killian. His blue eyes glittered with a feral light that frightened her. "All the trouble I'm causing..."

"I'm here to protect all of you," Killian said. "I'm going to try to get to the bottom of this mess as soon as possible."

With a sigh, Susannah nodded. "I felt it. The moment you were introduced to me, I felt safe."

"Well," Killian growled, rising to his feet, "I'd still stay alert. Paranoia's a healthy reaction to have until I can figure out if you're really safe or not," he said, setting the cup and saucer in the sink.

Grimly Killian placed his hands on the counter and stared out the window. The blue-and-white checked curtains at the window made it homey, and it was tempting to relax and absorb the feeling. He'd been so long without home and family, and he was rarely able to go back to Ireland to visit what was left of his family—Meg. Sadness moved through him, deep and cutting. Being here with Susannah and her family had been a reprieve of sorts from his loneliness.

"Sean, I really don't feel good about going back to town, back to my house, knowing all this." Susannah stared at his long, lean back. He was silhouetted against the dusk, his mouth a tight line holding back unknown emotions, perhaps pain. Overcoming her shyness, she whispered, "Now that I know the real reason you're here, I'll take you up on that offer to stay with me at night. If you want..."

Slowly Killian turned around. He groaned internally as he met her hope-filled gaze, saw her lips part. The driving urge to kiss her, to explore those wonderful lips, was nearly his undoing.

Susannah took his silence as a refusal. A strange light burned in his intense gaze. "Well...I mean, you don't have to. I don't want you to feel like a—"

"I'll stay," he muttered abruptly.

Nervously Susannah stood and wiped her damp hands down her thighs. "Are you sure?" He looked almost angry. With her? Since the assault, she'd lost so much of her self-esteem. Susannah found herself quivering like jelly inside; it was a feeling she'd never experienced before that fateful night at the bus station.

"Yes," Killian snapped, moving toward the back door. "I'll get my gear down at your folks' place and bring it up here."

Feeling as if she'd done something wrong, Susannah watched him leave. And then she upbraided herself for that feeling. It was a victim's response, according to the woman therapist who had counseled her a number of times when she'd come out of the coma but was still at the hospital.

"Stop it," Susannah sternly told herself. "If he's angry, ask him why. Don't assume it's because of something you said." As she moved to the bedroom next to her own, separated by the only bathroom in the house, Susannah felt a gamut of insecurities. When Sean returned, she was determined to find out the truth of why he'd been so abrupt with her.

Chapter Five

"Are you angry with me?" Susannah asked Killian, the words coming out more breathless than forceful, to her dismay. He'd just dropped his leather bag in the spare bedroom.

Turning, he scowled. "No. Why?"

"You acted upset earlier. I just wanted to know if it was aimed at me."

Straightening, Killian moved to where Susannah stood, at the entrance to his bedroom. Twilight had invaded the depths of the old house, and her sober features were strained. It hurt to think that she thought he was angry with her. Roughly he said, "My being upset has nothing to do with you, Susannah."

"What does it have to do with, then?"

He grimaced, unwilling to comment.

"I know you didn't want this assignment from Morgan...."

Exasperated, he muttered, "Not at first." Killian refused to acknowledge that Susannah appealed to him on some primal level of himself. Furthermore, he couldn't allow himself to get involved emotionally with the person he had to protect. And that was why he had never before accepted an assignment involving a woman; his weakness centered around those who were least able to protect themselves—the women of the world. Emotions touched him deeply, and there was little he could do to parry them, because they always hit him hard, no matter what he tried to do to avoid them. Men were far easier to protect; they were just as closed up as he was, lessening the emotional price tag.

Susannah wasn't about to let Killian squirm out of the confrontation. "I learned a long time ago to talk out problems. Maybe that's a woman's way, but men can profit from it, too." She lifted her hands and held his scrutinizing gaze, gaining confidence. "I don't want you here if you don't want to be, Sean. I hate thinking I'm a burden to anyone."

The ache to reach out and tame a strand of hair away from her flushed features was excruciatingly tempting. Killian exhaled loudly. "I wish you weren't so sensitive to other people's moods."

She smiled a little. "Maybe it's because I work with handicapped children who often either can't speak or have trouble communicating in general. I can't help it. What's bothering you, Sean?"

He shoved his hands into the pockets of his jeans and studied her tautly. "It's my nature not to talk," he warned.

"It does take courage to talk," Susannah agreed, gathering her own courage, determined to get to the root of his problem with her. "It's easier to button up and retreat into silence," she said more firmly.

His mouth had become nothing more than a slash. "Let's drop this conversation."

Susannah stood in the doorway, feeling the tension radiating from him. He not only looked dangerous, he felt dangerous. Her mouth grew dry. "No."

The one word, softly spoken, struck him solidly. "I learned a long time ago to say nothing. I'm a man with a lot of ugly secrets, Susannah. Secrets I'm not proud of. They're best left unsaid."

"I don't agree," Susannah replied gently. She saw the terror lurking in the depths of Killian's eyes as he avoided her searching gaze. "My folks helped me through the worst of my reactions after I came out of the coma. They understood my need to talk about my fears by writing them down on a piece of paper when I couldn't speak." She blinked uncertainly. "I couldn't even cry, Sean. The tears just wouldn't come. The horrible humiliation I felt—still feel even now—was lessened because they cared enough to listen, to hold me when I was so scared. At least I had someone who cared how I felt, who cried *for* me when the pain was too much for me to bear alone."

Killian lifted his chin and stared deeply into her luminous gray eyes. The need to confide, to open his arms and sweep her against him, was painfully real. His whole body was tense with pain. "In my line of work, there aren't many therapists available when things start coming down—or falling apart. There are no safe havens, Susannah. To avoid trouble and ensure safety, I breathe through my nose. It keeps my mouth shut."

He'd said too much already. Killian looked around, wanting to escape, but Susannah stood stubbornly in the doorway, barring any exit. Panic ate at him.

Susannah shook her head. "I felt such sadness around you," she whispered, opening her hands to him. "You put on such a frightening mask, Sean—"

Angrily he rasped, "Back off."

The words slapped her. His tone had a lethal quality. Swallowing hard, Susannah saw fear, mixed with anguish, mirrored in his narrowed eyes. The words had been spoken in desperation, not anger. "How can I? I feel how uncomfortable you are here with me. I feel as if I've done something to make you feel like that." She raised her eyes to the ceiling. "Sean, I can't live like that with a person. How can you?"

Nostrils flaring, Killian stared at her in disbelief. Her honesty was bone deep—a kind he'd rarely encountered. Killian didn't dare tell her the raw, blatant truth—that he wanted her in every way imaginable. "I guess I've been out in the field too long," he told her in a low, growling tone. "I'm used to harshness, Susannah, not the softness a woman has, not a home. Being around you is...different...and I'm having to adjust." *A lot.*

"And," he added savagely, seeing how flustered she was becoming, "I'm used to bunking with men, not a woman. I get nightmares." When her face fell with compassion for him, he couldn't deal with it—almost hating her for it, for forcing the feelings out of him. "The night is my enemy, Susannah. And it's an enemy for anyone who might be near me when it happens. The past comes back," he warned thickly. Killian wanted to protect Susannah from that dark side of himself. He was afraid he might not be able to control himself, that terrorized portion of him that sometimes trapped him for hours in its brutal grip, ruling him.

Standing there absorbing the emotional pain contained in his admission, Susannah realized for the first time that Killian was terribly human. He wasn't the superman she'd first thought, although Morgan's men had a proud reputation for being exactly that. The discovery was as breathtaking as it was disturbing. She had no experience with a man like Killian—someone who had been grievously wounded by a world whose existence she could hardly fathom. The pleading look Killian gave her, the twist of his lips as he shared the information with her, tore at Susannah's heart. Instinctively she realized that Killian needed to be held, too. If only for a little while. He needed a safe haven from the stormy dangers inherent in his chosen profession. That was something she could give him while he stayed with her.

"I understand," she whispered unsteadily. "And if you have bad dreams, I'll come out and make you a cup of tea. Maybe we can talk about it."

He slowly raised his head, feeling the tension make his joints ache. He held Susannah's guileless eyes, eyes that were filled with hope. "Your naiveté nearly got you killed once," he rasped. "Just stay away from me if you hear me up and moving around at night, Susannah. *Stay away.*"

She gave him a wary look, seeing the anguish in his narrowed eyes even as they burned with desire. Desire for her? Susannah wished that need could be for her alone, but she knew Killian was the kind of man who allowed no grass to grow under his feet. He was a wanderer over the face of the earth, with no interest in settling down. Much as she hated to admit it, she had to be honest with herself.

Killian wasn't going to say anything else, Susannah realized. She stepped back into the hallway, at a loss. Lamely she held his hooded stare.

"It's as if you're saying you're a danger to me."

"I am."

Susannah shook her head. "I wish," she said softly, "I had more experience with the world, with men..."

Killian wanted to move to her and simply enfold Susannah in his arms. She looked confused and bereft. "Stay the way you are," he told her harshly. "You don't want to know what the world can offer."

Susannah wasn't so sure. She felt totally unprepared to deal with a complex man like Sean, yet she was powerfully drawn to him. "Should I follow my normal schedule of doing things around here tomorrow morning?" At least this was a safe topic of conversation.

"Yes."

"I see. Good night, Sean."

"Good night." The words came out in a rasp. Killian tasted his frustration, and felt a heated longing coil through him. Susannah looked crestfallen. Could he blame her? No. Darkness was complete now, and he automatically perused the gloomy area. Perhaps talking a little bit about himself hadn't been so bad after all. At least with her. He knew he couldn't live under the same roof without warning Susannah of his violent night world.

By ten, Killian was in bed, wearing only his pajama bottoms. He stared blankly at the plaster ceiling, which was in dire need of repair. His senses functioned like radar, swinging this way and that, picking up nuances of sound and smell. Nothing seemed out of place, so he relaxed to a degree. And then, against his will, his attention shifted to dwell on Susannah. She had a surprisingly stubborn side to her—and he liked discovering that strength within her. Outwardly she might seem soft and naive, but she had emotional convictions that served as the roots of her strength.

Glancing at the only window in his room, Killian could see stars dotting the velvet black of the sky. Everything was so peaceful here. Another layer of tension dissolved around him, and he found himself enjoying the old double bed, the texture of the clean cotton sheets that Susannah had made the bed with, and the symphony of the crickets chirping outside the house.

What was it about this place that permeated his constant state of wariness and tension to make him relax to this degree? Killian had no answers, or at least none he was willing to look at closely. Exhausted, he knew he had to try to get some sleep. He moved restlessly on the bed, afraid of what the night might hold. He forced his eyes closed, inhaled deeply and drifted off to sleep. On the nightstand was his pistol, loaded and with the safety off, perpetually at the ready.

* * *

Killian jerked awake, his hand automatically moving to his pistol. Sunlight streamed through the window and the lacy pale green curtains. Blinking, he slowly sat up and shoved several locks of hair off his brow. The scent of freshly brewed coffee and frying bacon wafted on the air. He inhaled hungrily and threw his legs across the creaky bed. Relief flowed through him as he realized that for once the nightmares hadn't come to haunt him. Puzzled, he moved to the bathroom. Not only had the nightmares stayed at bay, but he'd slept very late. Usually his sleep was punctuated by moments of stark terror throughout the night and he finally fell more heavily asleep near dawn. Still, he never slept past six—ever. But now it was eight o'clock. Stymied about why he'd slept so late, he stepped into a hot shower.

Dressed in a white shirt and jeans, Killian swung out of his room and down the hall, following the enticing smells emanating from the kitchen. Halting in the doorway, he drank in the sight of Susannah working over the old wood stove. Today she wore a sleeveless yellow blouse, well-worn jeans and white tennis shoes. Her hair, thick and abundant, cloaked her shoulders. As if she had sensed his presence, she looked up.

"I thought this might get you out of bed." She grinned. "So much for keeping up with me and my schedule. I was up at five-thirty, and you were still sawing logs."

Rubbing his face, Killian managed a sheepish look as he headed for the counter where the coffeepot sat. "I overslept," he muttered.

Taking the bacon out of the skillet and placing it on a paper towel to soak up the extra grease, Susannah smiled. "Don't worry, your secrets are safe with me."

Killian gave her a long, absorbing look, thinking how pretty she looked this morning. But he noted a slight puffiness beneath Susannah's eyes and wondered if she'd been crying. "I guess I'll have to get used to this," he rasped. The coffee was strong, hot and black—just the way he liked it. Susannah placed a stack of pancakes, the rasher of bacon and a bottle of maple syrup before him and sat down opposite him.

"'This' meaning me?"

Killian dug hungrily into the pancakes. "It's everything."

Susannah sat back and shook her head. "One- or two-word answers, Sean. I swear. What do you mean by 'everything'?"

He gave her a brief look. He was really enjoying the buckwheat pancakes. "It's been a long time since I was in a home, not a house," he told her between bites.

She ate slowly, listening closely not only to what he said, but also to how he said it. "So, home life appeals to you after all?"

He raised his brows.

"I thought," Susannah offered, "that you were a rolling stone that gathered no moss. A man with wanderlust in his soul."

He refused to hold her warm gaze. "Home means everything to me." The pancakes disappeared in a hurry, and the bacon quickly followed. Killian took his steaming cup of coffee and tipped his chair back on two legs. The kitchen fragrances lingered like perfume, and birds sang cheerfully outside the screen door, enhancing his feeling of contentment. Susannah looked incredibly lovely, and Killian thought he was in heaven—or as close as the likes of him was ever going to get to it.

Sipping her coffee, Susannah risked a look at Killian. "To me, a house is built of walls and beams. A home is built with love and dreams. You said you were from Ireland. Were you happy over there?"

Uncomfortable, Killian shrugged. "Northern Ireland isn't exactly a happy place to live." He shot her a hard look. "I learned early on, Susannah, the danger of caring about someone too much, because they'd be ripped away from me."

It felt as if a knife were being thrust down through Susannah. She gripped the delicate cup hard between her hands. "But what—"

With a shrug, Killian tried to cover up his own unraveling emotions. Gruffly he said, "That was the past—there's no need to rehash it. This is the present."

Pain for Killian settled over Susannah. She didn't know what had happened to him as a child, but his words "the danger of caring about someone too much" created a knot in her stomach.

Finishing her coffee, Susannah quietly got up and gathered the plates and flatware. At the counter, she began washing the dishes in warm, soapy water.

Killian rose and moved to where Susannah stood. He spotted a towel hanging on a nail and began to dry the dishes as she rinsed them.

"You're upset."

"No."

"You don't lie well at all. Your voice is a dead give-away—not to mention those large, beautiful eyes of yours." No one could have been more surprised than Killian at what had just transpired. He hadn't meant to allude to the tragedy. Her empathy was touching, but Killian knew that to feel another person's pain at that depth was dangerous. Why didn't Susannah shield herself more from him?

Avoiding his sharpened gaze, Susannah concentrated on washing the dishes. "It's just that, well, you seem to carry a lot of pain." She inhaled shakily.

"I told you the secrets I carried weren't good ones," he warned her darkly.

"Yes, you did. . . ." she agreed softly.

Disgusted with himself, Killian muttered, "Face it, life isn't very nice."

Susannah's hands stilled in the soothing water. Lifting her chin, she met and held his stormy gaze. "I don't believe that. There's always hope," she challenged.

With a muffled sound, Killian suppressed the curse that rose to his lips. Susannah didn't deserve his harsh side, his survival reflexes. "*Hope* isn't a word I recognize."

"What about dreams?"

His smile was deadly. Cynical. "Dreams? More like nightmares, colleen."

There was no way to parry the grim finality of his view of the world—at least not yet. Susannah softened her voice. "Well, perhaps the time you spend here will change your mind."

"A month or so in Eden before I descend back into hell? Be careful, Susannah. You don't want to invest anything in me. I live in hell. I don't want to pull you into it.''

A chill moved through her. His lethal warning sounded as if it came from the very depths of his injured, untended soul. Killian was like a wounded animal—hurting badly, lashing out in pain. Rallying, Susannah determined not to allow Killian to see how much his warning had shaken her.

''Well,'' she went on with forced lightness, ''you'll probably be terribly bored sooner or later. In the end, you'll be more than ready to leave.''

Killian scowled as he continued to dry the flatware one piece at a time. ''We'll see'' was all he'd say. He'd said enough. *Too much.* The crestfallen look in Susannah's eyes made him want to cry. Cry! Struck by his cruelty toward her, Killian would have done anything to take back his words. Susannah had gone through enough hell of her own without him dumping his sordid past on her, too.

''What's on the list this morning?'' he demanded abruptly.

Susannah tried to gather her strewn, shocked feelings. ''Weeding the garden. I try to do it during the morning hours, while it's still cool. We have to pick the slugs off, weed and check the plants for other insects. That sort of thing.'' Again, tension vibrated around Killian, and it translated to her. She knew there was a slight wobble in her strained tone. Had Killian picked it up? Susannah didn't have the courage to glance at him as he continued drying dishes.

A huge part of Susannah wanted to help heal his wounds. Her heart told her she had the ability to do just that. Hadn't she helped so many children win freedom from crosses they'd been marked to bear for life? She'd helped guide them out of trapped existences with color, paints and tempera. Each year she saw a new batch of special children, and by June they were smiling far more than when they'd first come to class. No, there was hope for Killian, whether he wanted to admit it or not.

Killian methodically pulled the weeds that poked their heads up between the rows of broccoli, cauliflower and tomatoes. A few rows over, Susannah worked, an old straw hat protecting her from the sun's intensity. He worked bareheaded, absorbing energy from the sunlight. Since their conversation in the kitchen that morning, she'd been suspiciously silent, and it needled Killian enormously.

He had to admit, there was something pleasurable about thrusting his hands into the damp, rich soil. Over near the fence, the baby robin that had previously fallen out of its nest chirped loudly for its parents to bring her more food. Killian wore his shoulder holster, housing the Beretta beneath his left arm. Susannah had given him a disgruntled look when he'd put on the shoulder harness, but had said nothing. Just as well. He didn't want her getting any ideas about saving him and his dark, hopeless soul. Let her realize who and what he was. That way, she'd keep her distance. He wasn't worth saving.

Susannah got off her hands and knees. She took the handful of slugs she'd found and placed them on the other side of the fence, under the fruit tree, below the robin's nest. Not believing in insecticides, she tried to use nature's balance to maintain her gardens. The robins would feed the slugs to their babies, completing the natural cycle.

Usually her work relaxed her, but this morning the silence between her and Killian was terribly strained, and she had no idea how to lessen it. She glanced over at Killian, who worked in a crouch, pulling weeds, his face set. Every once in a while, she could feel him surveying the area, his guarded watchfulness evident.

Susannah took off her hat, wiped her damp brow with the back of her hand and walked toward the house. She wanted to speak to him, but she felt that cold wall around him warning her to leave him alone.

Entering the kitchen, Susannah realized just how lonely was the world Killian lived in. It was sheer agony for him to talk. Each conversation was like pulling teeth—painful and nerve-racking. Tossing her straw hat on the table, Susannah poured two tall, icy glasses of lemonade.

Killian entered silently, catching her off guard. Susannah's heart hammered briefly. His face was glistening with sweat, but his mouth was no longer pursed, she noted, and his eyes looked lighter—almost happy, if she was reading him accurately.

"Come on, sit down. You've earned a rest," she said.

The lemonade disappeared in a hurry as he gulped it down and nodded his thanks.

"More?"

"Please." Killian sat at the table, his hands folded on top of it, watching Susannah move with her incredible natural grace.

With another nod of appreciation, he took the newly filled glass but this time didn't gulp it down. He glanced at his watch. "I hadn't realized two hours had gone by."

Susannah smiled tentatively. Casting about for some safe topic, she waved at the colorful pictures on the kitchen walls. "My most recent class did these. Some of the kids are mentally retarded, others have had deformities since birth. They range in intellectual age from about six to twelve. I love drawing them out of their shells." And then, deliberately holding his gaze, she added, "They find happiness by making the most of what they have." Susannah pointed again to the tempera paintings that she'd had framed. "I keep these because they're before-and-after drawings," she confided warmly.

"Oh?"

"The paintings on this wall were done when the children first came to class in September. The paintings on the right were done just before school was out in June. Take a look."

Killian rose and went over to the paintings, his glass of lemonade in hand. One child's first painting was dark and shadowy—the one done nine months later was bright and sunny in comparison. Another painting had a boy in a wheelchair looking glum. In the next, he was smiling and waving to the birds overhead. Killian glanced at Susannah over his shoulder. "Telling, aren't they?"

"Very."

He studied the others in silence. Finally he turned around, came back to the table and sat down. "You must have the patience of Job."

With a little laugh, Susannah shook her head. "For me, it's a wonderful experience watching these kids open up and discover happiness—some of them for the first time in their lives.'' Her voice took on more feeling. ''Just watching them blossom, learn to trust, to explore, means everything to me. It's a real privilege for me.''

''I guess some people pursue happiness and others create it. I envy those kids.'' Killian swallowed convulsively, feeling uncomfortably as if her sparkling eyes were melting his hardened heart—and his hardened view of the world. Her lower lip trembled under the intensity of his stare, and the overwhelming need to reach over, to pull Susannah to his chest and kiss her until she molded to him with desire, nearly unstrung his considerable control. If he stayed at the table, he'd touch her. He'd kiss the hell out of her.

Susannah wanted Sean to get used to the idea that he, too, could have happiness. ''You know, what we did out there this morning made you happy. I could see it in your eyes. Your face is relaxed. Isn't that something?''

Leaving her side abruptly, Killian placed his empty glass on the counter, a little more loudly than necessary. ''What's next? What do you want me to do?''

Shocked, Susannah watched the hardness come back into Killian's features. She'd pushed him too far. ''I... Well, the screen in my bedroom could be fixed....'' she said hesitantly.

''Then what?'' A kind of desperation ate at Killian. He didn't dare stay in such close proximity to Susannah. The more she revealed of herself, the more she trusted him with her intimate thoughts and feelings, the more she threatened his much-needed defenses. Dammit, she trusted too easily!

"Then lunch. I was going to make us lunch, and then I thought we'd pick the early snow peas and freeze them this afternoon," she said.

"Fine."

Blinking, Susannah watched Killian stalk out of the kitchen. The tension was back in him; he was like a trap that begged to be sprung. Shakily she drew in a breath, all too clearly recognizing that the unbidden hunger in his eyes was aimed directly at her. Suddenly she felt like an animal in a hunter's sights.

Chapter Six

"Look out!" Killian's shriek careened around the darkened bedroom. He jerked himself upright, his hand automatically moving for the pistol. Cool metal met his hot, sweaty fingers. Shadows from the past danced around him. His breathing was ragged and chaotic. The roar of rifles and the blast of mortars flashed in front of his wide, glazed eyes as he sat rigidly in bed. A hoarse cry, almost a sob, tore from his contorted lips.

He made a muffled sound of disgust. With the back of his hand, Killian wiped his eyes clear of tears. Where was he? What room? What country? Peru? Algeria? Laos? *Where?*

His chest rising and falling rapidly, Killian narrowed his eyes as he swung his gaze around the quiet room. It took precious seconds for him to realize that he was here, in Kentucky. Cursing softly, he leaped out of bed, his pajama bottoms damp with sweat and clinging to his taut body. Shaking. He was shaking. It was nothing new. Often he would shake for a good hour after coming awake. More important, the nightmare hadn't insidiously kept control of him after waking. The flashbacks frightened him for Susannah's sake.

Laying the pistol down, Killian rubbed his face savagely, trying to force the remnants of the nightmare away. What he needed to shock him back into the present was a brutally cold shower. That and a fortifying cup of coffee. Forcing himself to move on wobbly legs, he made it to the bathroom. Fumbling for the shower faucet, he found it and turned it on full-force.

Later, he padded down the darkened hall in his damp, bare feet, a white towel draped low around his hips. His watch read 3:00 a.m.—the same time he usually had the nightmares. Shoving damp strands of hair off his brow, he rounded the corner. Shock riveted him to the spot.

"I thought you might like some coffee," Susannah whispered unsteadily. She was standing near the counter in a long white cotton nightgown. Her hands were clasped in front of her. "That and some company?"

Rubbing his mouth with the back of his hand, Killian stood tautly, his heightened senses reeling with impact. Moonlight lovingly caressed Susannah, the luminescence outlining her slender shape through her thin cotton gown. The lace around the gown's boat neck emphasized her collarbones and her slender neck. He gulped and allowed his hand to fall back to his side. Susannah's face looked sleepy, her eyes dreamy with a softness that aroused a longing in him to bury himself in her, hotly, deeply. She remained perfectly still as he devoured her with his starving gaze.

There was fear in her eyes, mixed with desire and longing. Killian not only saw it in the nuances of her fleeting expression, but sensed it, as well. Like a wolf too long without a mate, he ached to claim her as his own. And then, abruptly he laughed at himself. Who was he kidding? She was all the things he was not. She had hope. She believed in a future filled with dreams. Hell, she gave handicapped children back the chance to dream.

"It's not a good time to be around me," he rasped.

Inhaling shakily, Susannah nodded. "It's a chance I'll take." Never had she seen a man of such power, intensity and beauty as Killian. He stood in the kitchen doorway, the towel draped casually across his lean hips, accentuating his near nakedness.

Killian's shoulders were proudly thrown back, and his muscles were cleanly delineated. His chest was covered with hair that headed like an arrow down his long torso and flat belly. The dark line of hair disappeared beneath the stark whiteness of the towel, but still, little was left to the imagination. Susannah gulped convulsively.

Susannah's skin tingled where his hungry gaze had swept across her. Trying to steady her desire for him, she noticed that her hands shook as she turned to put the coffee into the pot.

It had taken everything for Susannah to tear her gaze from his overwhelming masculine image. "I—I heard you scream. At first I thought it was a nightmare I was having, and then I realized it wasn't me screaming. It was you."

Killian remained frozen in the doorway. The husky softness of Susannah's voice began to dissolve some of the terror that seemed to twist within him like a living being.

She shrugged. "I didn't know what to do."

"You did the right thing," he said raggedly. He forced himself to move toward the table. Gripping the chair, he sat down, afraid he might fall down if he didn't. His knees were still weak from the virulent nightmare. He looked up at Susannah. "Didn't I tell you that I wasn't worth the risk? Look at you. You're shaking." And she was. He wanted desperately to reassure her somehow, but he couldn't.

Rubbing her arms, Susannah nodded. "I'll be okay."

Killian felt like hell. He'd scared her, triggered the fear she'd barely survived months ago, and he knew it. "I walk around in a living death every day of my life. You don't deserve to be around it—or me."

The sweat glistening on Killian's taut muscles spoke to her of the hell he was still caught up in. Susannah forced herself to move through her fear and cross to his side. She reached out and gently laid her hands on his shoulders.

Killian groaned. Her touch was so warm, so steadying.

"Just sit there," she whispered in a strained tone. "Let me work the knots out of your shoulders. You're so tense."

He opened his mouth to protest, but the kneading quality of her strong, slender hands as they worked his aching muscles stopped him. Instead of speaking, he closed his eyes and gradually began to relax. With each sliding, coaxing movement of her fingers along his skin, a little more of the fear he carried with him dissolved. Eventually he allowed himself to sag against the chair.

"Lean on me," Susannah coaxed. She pressed her hand to his sweaty brow and guided his head against her.

How easy it was to have his head cushioned against her as her hands moved with confidence on his shoulders and neck. A ragged sigh issued from him, and he closed his eyes, trusting her completely.

"Good," she crooned softly, watching his short, spiky lashes droop closed. Even his mouth, once a harsh line holding back a deluge of emotions, gradually relaxed.

Susannah felt the steel-cable strength of his muscles beneath her hands. He was built like a cougar—lean and lithe. Her feelings were alive, bright and clamoring not only for acknowledgment, but for action. The thrill of touching Killian, of having him trust her this much, was dizzying and inviting. Susannah ached to lean forward and place a soft kiss on his furrowed brow. How much pain did this man carry within him?

As she stood in the moonlit kitchen with him, massaging his terror and tension away, Susannah realized that Killian's life must have been one of unending violence.

"Two years ago," she said unsteadily as she smoothed away the last of the rigidity from his now-supple muscles, "I had a little boy, Stevey, in my class.

He was mentally retarded and had been taken from his home by Social Services. He was only eight years old, and he was like a frightened little animal. The social worker told me that his father was an alcoholic and his mother was on drugs. They both beat up on him.''

Killian's eyes snapped open.

"I'm telling you this for a reason," Susannah whispered, her hands stilling on his shoulders. "At first, Stevey would only crawl into a corner and hide. Gradually I earned his trust, and then I got him to draw. The pictures told me so much about what he'd endured, what he'd suffered through, alone and unprotected. There wasn't a day that went by that I didn't cry for him.

"Stevey taught me more about trust and love than any other person in my life ever has. Gradually, throughout the year that he was in my class, he came to life. He truly blossomed, and it was so breathtaking. He learned to smile, then to laugh. His new foster parents love him deeply, and that helped bring him out of the terror and humiliation he'd endured.

"I saw this frightened, beaten child have enough blind faith in another human being to rally and reach out just once more. Stevey had a kind of courage that I feel is the rarest kind in the world, and the hardest to acquire." Susannah reached out and stroked Killian's damp hair. "Stevey knew only violence, broken trust and heartache. But something in him—his spirit, if you will—had the strength to work through all of that and embrace others who truly loved him and accepted him for who he was."

Killian released a shaky breath, wildly aware of Susannah's trembling fingers lightly caressing his hair.

Did she realize what she was doing? Did she know that if she kept it up he'd take her hard and fast, burying himself in her hot depths? Longing warred with control. He eased out of her hands and sat up.

"Why don't you get us that coffee?" he said. His voice was none too steady, and it had a sandpaper rasp. Glancing up as Susannah walked past him, he saw her face. How could she look so damned angelic when all he felt was his blood pounding like a dam ready to burst?

Miraculously, the nightmare and its contents had disappeared beneath Susannah's gentle, questing hands. Killian's eyes slitted as he studied her at the counter, where she was pouring the coffee. What was it about her? Grateful that she wasn't looking at him, Killian struggled to get his raging need back under control. Usually he had no problem disconnecting himself from his volcanic emotions, but Susannah aroused him to a white heat of desire.

With trembling hands, Susannah set the coffee before Killian, sharply conscious of his perusal of her. His words, his warning, kept thrumming through her. She felt danger and intensity surrounding them. Did she have the courage to stay? To be there for Killian? Forcing herself to look up, she met and held his blue gaze, a gaze that was hooded with some unknown emotion that seemed to melt her inwardly.

Gulping, she sat down at his elbow, determined not to allow him to scare her away. Right now, her heart counseled her, he needed a friend, someone he could talk with.

Killian sat there thunderstruck. Susannah couldn't be this naive—she must realize how he wanted her. Yet she sat down next to him, her face filled with determination as she sipped her steaming coffee. Angry, and feeling at war within himself, he snapped irritably, "Why don't you go back to bed?"

"Because you need me here."

His eyes widened enormously.

Prepared to risk everything, Susannah met and held his incredulous gaze. "You need a friend, Sean."

His fingers gripped his cup, and he stared down at the black contents. "Talking is the last thing I want to do right now."

She tried to absorb his brutal, angry words. "What, then?"

He snapped a look at her. "Get away from me, Susannah, while you can. Stop trying to get close. I'm not Stevey. I'm a grown man, with a grown man's needs. You're in danger. Stay, and I can't answer for what I might do."

There was such anguish in his raspy words, and she felt his raw need of her. She sat up, her fingers releasing the cup. "No, you aren't like Stevey," Susannah whispered unsteadily. "But you are wounded—and in need of a safe haven."

With a hiss, Killian jerked to his feet, the chair nearly tipping over from the swiftness of his movement. "Wounded animals can bite those who try to help them!" Breathing harshly, he walked to the other end of the kitchen. "Dammit, Susannah, stay away from me. You've already been hurt by a man who nearly killed you." He struck his chest. "I can hurt you in so many different ways. Is that what you want? Do you want me to take you, to bury myself in you, to make night and day merge into one until you don't know anything except me, my arms, my body and—''

With a muffled sound, Killian spun around, jerked open the screen door and disappeared into the night. If he didn't go, he was going to take Susannah right there on the hard wooden floor. The primal blood was racing through him, blotting out reason, disintegrating his control. As he stalked off the porch, he knew she was an innocent in this. She was the kind of woman he'd always dreamed of—but then, dreams never could stand the test of harsh daylight.

Who was he kidding? Killian walked swiftly, his feet and ankles soon soaked from the trail he made through the dewy grass. Moonlight shifted across him in unending patterns as he continued his blind walk through the orchard. He had to protect Susannah from himself—at all costs. She didn't deserve to get tangled up with his kind. It could only end in disaster.

Gradually he slowed his pace as his head began to clear. The night was cool, but not chilly. He realized with disgust that he'd left without his weapon, and that he'd left Susannah wide open to attack if someone was prowling around. As he halted and swiftly shifted his awareness to more external things, he acknowledged that, although unarmed, he was never defenseless. No, he'd been taught to kill a hundred different ways without need of any kind of weapon.

He stood in the middle of the orchard, scowling. Bats dipped here and there, chasing after choice insects that he couldn't see. The old homestead was a quarter of a mile away, looking broken down and in dire need of paint, and also the love and care it would take to put it back in good repair. Killian laughed harshly. Wasn't he just like that old house? The only difference was that the scars he wore were mostly carried on the inside, where no one could see them. No one except Susannah. Why couldn't she be like everyone else and see only the tough exterior he presented to the world?

Killian stood there a long time, mulling over the story she'd told him about the little boy named Stevey. The boy deserved Susannah's loving care. She was the right person to help coax him out of his dark shell of fear. Her words, soft and strained, floated back to him: "You are wounded—and need a safe haven."

How long he stood there thinking about their conversation, he didn't know. When he glanced at his watch, it was 4:00 a.m. Forcing himself, he walked slowly back to the homestead. As he walked, he prayed—something he rarely did—that Susannah had had enough sense to go back to bed. What would he do if she was still up and waiting for him? His mouth was dry, and he wiped at it with the back of his hand. He didn't know.

Susannah was out in the extensive rose garden, giving the colorful flowers the special food that helped them to bloom. It was nearly noon, and she was hot, even though she wore her straw hat, a sleeveless white blouse and a threadbare pair of jeans. Her mind and heart centered on Killian. She'd gone back to bed around four, and had promptly plummeted into a deep, restful sleep. When she'd gotten up this morning at six, his bedroom door had been shut. Was he in there? Had he gone somewhere else? Susannah didn't know, and she hadn't had the courage to find out.

Taking her one-gallon bucket and the box of rose food, she went back over to the hose to mix the ingredients for the next rosebush. The air was heavy with the wonderful fragrance of the flowering bushes. The rose garden sat on the southern side of the homestead, where there was the most light. There was no fence around it, and the bushes stretched for nearly a quarter of a mile.

Susannah hunched over the bucket and poured the rose food into the pooling water, stirring it with her hand. The water turned a pretty pink color. Pink always reminded her of love, she thought mildly. Then Killian's harsh warning pounded back through her. He *was* dangerous, she thought, feeling the heat of longing flow through her—dangerous to her heart, to her soul. Killian had the ability to touch her very essence. How, she didn't know. She only knew he had that capacity, and no other man she'd ever met had been able to touch her so deeply.

Shutting off the faucet, Susannah set the food aside and hefted the gallon bucket to carry it to the next rosebush, a beautiful lavender one with at least ten blossoms. No longer could she keep from entertaining the idea of loving Killian. Her dreams had turned torrid toward morning, and she vividly recalled images of his hands caressing her body, his mouth ravishing her with wild abandon, meeting her willing, equally hungry lips.

She poured the bucket's contents into the well around the rosebush. What did she want? *Killian.* Why? Because... Susannah straightened and put the bucket aside. She pulled out a pair of scissors and began pruning off old blooms. Was it to help him heal?

Yes. To show him that another person could trust him fully, fearlessly, even if he didn't trust himself? Yes. To give him her love in hopes that he might overcome his own fear of loving and losing—and to love her? *Yes*.

Stymied, she stood there, her hands cupped around one of the large lavender roses. She leaned forward, inhaling the delicate fragrance. Life was so beautiful. Why couldn't Killian see that? As she studied the many-petaled bloom, Susannah ached for him. She knew she had the ability to show him the beauty of life. But what then? He would be in her life only long enough to catch the killer who might be stalking her. He'd repeatedly warned her that he wasn't worth loving.

But he was. With a sigh, Susannah pocketed the scissors, picked up the bucket and headed back to the faucet. Her stomach growled, and she realized that it was nearly lunchtime and she was hungry. Placing all the gardening tools near the spigot, Susannah walked back to the homestead. Would Killian be there? And if he was, would he be up yet? Fear mingled with need of him inside her. How would she handle their next confrontation?

Killian's head snapped up at the sound of someone's approach. He was at the kitchen cabinets, searching through them for something to eat. He'd just gotten up and taken a scaldingly hot shower to awaken, then gotten dressed in a dark blue short-sleeved shirt and jeans. He felt like someone had poleaxed him.

Susannah opened the screen door and took off her straw hat. When she saw him, she hesitated.

Killian glared at her.

"Hungry?" she asked, hoping to hide the tension she felt. She continued into the room and placed her hat on the table.

"Like a bear," he muttered, moving away from the counter.

Susannah kept plenty of distance between them. She noticed the stormy quality in his blue eyes, and her nerves grew taut. Scared, but aware that Killian needed courage from her, not cowardice, Susannah said firmly, "Have a seat and I'll fix you what I'm going to have: a tuna sandwich, sweet pickles and pretzels."

Sitting down, Killian tried to soften his growly bad humor. "Okay."

"Coffee or iced tea?"

"I don't care."

Gathering her dissolving courage, Susannah said, "I think you need a strong cup of coffee. Are you always like this when you wake up?" Killian looked fiercely unhappy, his eyes bleak, with dark circles under them. It was obvious he hadn't slept well after their verbal battle last night.

Killian refused to watch her as she moved to the icebox. "I told you I was a bastard."

She forced a laugh and brought bread and a bowl of prepared tuna to the counter. "You really aren't, you know. You're just grouchy because you lost some sleep last night and you haven't had your coffee yet."

"Maybe you're right." Killian watched her hungrily, every movement, every sway of her hips. Susannah had her sable hair swept into a ponytail, as usual, and it shone with each step she took. Her face glowed with the good health of a woman who loved the outdoors. Unhappily Killian folded his hands on the table. Why wouldn't Susannah heed his warning? Why didn't she believe that he was a bastard, someone capable of hurting her badly? He didn't want to hurt her—not her, of all people.

Humming softly, Susannah made coffee, prepared the sandwiches and put together a wholesome lunch. When she turned around, Killian's rugged profile still reflected his unhappiness. He sat tensely, his mouth pursed.

"Here, start on the sandwich. Bears don't do well on empty stomachs."

Grateful for her teasing, he took the sandwich and began eating. But he didn't taste it—all he was aware of was his own intense suffering, and Susannah's sunlit presence. She chased away his gloom, that terrible shadow that always hovered over him like a vulture ready to rip out what little was left of his heart.

Placing the coffee before him, Susannah took her usual seat at his elbow. Her heart was hammering so hard in her chest that she feared Killian might hear it. As she forced herself to eat, the kitchen fell into a stilted silence.

"Earlier, I went down to visit my parents," she offered after a moment, trying to lessen the tension. "They told me my school had called, that the principal wanted me to consider coming back to work sooner." She picked up a pickle and frowned. "I really miss teaching. I have a new class of kids that I've never seen." She watched Killian raise his head, his blue gaze settling on her. Her pulse raced. Trying to continue to sound nonchalant, she added, "So I called Mr. Gains back—that's the principal—and told him I'd like to return."

"When?" The word came out sharp.

Wiping her hands on a napkin, Susannah said, "Next Monday. I feel well enough now."

Relief shattered through Killian. That, and terrible disappointment. Some stupid part of him actually had held out hope that Susannah would stay, would persevere with him and reach into his heart. Putting down the sandwich, he reached for the coffee. Gulping down a swallow, he burned his mouth.

"Does that mean you're moving back into town? Into your house?"

"I—I don't know." Susannah managed a small shrug. "I really miss my kids, Sean. But I don't know if I'm ready to be alone. Do you know what I mean?"

He nodded and dropped his gaze. "Yeah, I know what you mean."

"I've been doing a lot of thinking this morning, and I guess I'll try to go to work full-time. Mr. Gains said if I have any problems I can split the class and work only half days for a while, until I get back into the swing of things."

"Half a day is enough for now."

She shrugged, not sure.

"Susannah, you're still healing."

And the other half of the day would be spent here, in Killian's intense presence, reminding her constantly of her need of him as a man, a lover. "I don't know," she confided in a low voice.

He set the coffee cup down a little more loudly than he'd intended. Susannah winced. "You aren't ready for all of that yet. You've got to pace yourself. Comas do funny things to people. What if you get flashbacks? Periods of vertigo? Or what if you blank out? All those things could happen under stress. And going back into that classroom *is* stress."

Susannah stared at him, feeling his raw intensity, his care. "Being here with you is stress, too, Sean."

Gripping the cup, he growled, "I suppose it is. I'm not the world's best person to be near. Around you, I shoot off my mouth, and look what it's done."

A soft smile touched her lips, and she leaned over and rested her hand on his arm. "Sean, some kinds of stress aren't bad. I like talking with you, sharing with you. I don't consider it bad or harmful. I feel shutting up and retreating is far more damaging."

"You would," Killian muttered, but he really didn't mean it. Just the cool, steadying touch of her fingers on his arm sent waves of need pulsing through him.

"Everyone needs someone," Susannah whispered. "Your needs are no different than anyone else's."

He cocked his head. "Don't be so sure."

She smiled a little, feeling danger swirling around her. "I'm betting your bark is worse than your bite."

"Oh? Was that the way it was with Stevey?"

Susannah forced herself to release him. "At first, every time I came near him, he lashed out at me."

"And what did you do?"

"I'd lean down, pull him against me and just hold him."

Killian shut his eyes and drew in a deep, shaky breath. "I don't know what to make of you, Susannah. Why would anyone put themselves in the line of fire just to let someone else know that they weren't going to be hurt again?" He opened his eyes, searching her thoughtful gray ones.

"I believe we're all healers, Sean. We not only have the ability to heal ourselves, but to heal others, too. Stevey wanted to be healed. Each time I approached him, he struck out less and less, until finally, one day, he opened his arms to me. It was such a beautiful, poignant moment."

"He trusted you," Killian said flatly.

"Yes, he did."

"You're a catalyst."

"So are you," she said wryly, meeting his wary eyes.

Uncomfortable, Killian wanted to shift the conversation back to her. "So you're going to try class for a full day next Monday?"

"Yes."

"All right, I'll drive you to work and hang around, if you don't mind. I want to get the layout of your school, your classroom. If they've got a contract out on you—and we still don't know if they do or not—I want to have that school, its entrances and exits, in my head in case something comes down."

She sat back, surprised. "Do you really think I'm in danger?"

"Until I can prove otherwise," Killian said roughly, "I'm assuming there's a hit man out there somewhere, just waiting for you. What you can't comprehend is that a contract means anytime, anywhere. A killer doesn't care where the hit takes place. He's been paid to do a job, and he's going to do it. He doesn't care if other lives get in the way."

The brutal harshness of his words sank into Susannah with a frightening chill. "What about my kids? Are they safe?"

Killian shrugged. "I don't know, Susannah. Hit men usually try for a clean one-shot deal. They don't like putting themselves in a messy situation where they could get caught." He saw the color drain from her face. "Look," he added harshly, "let me worry about the possibility of a hit man, okay? I know where to look, I know their usual methods. You'll be safe. And so will your kids," he added, softening his voice for her sake.

Getting up, Susannah moved to the counter. "I—I just didn't realize, Sean...."

"I didn't want you to," he muttered. "It's fairly easy to watch you here, at the farm. But the moment you start driving to work, shopping and doing all the other things normal people do daily, you become more of a target-rich opportunity."

She shivered at the military jargon. *Target-rich opportunity.* Gripping the cool porcelain of the double sink, she hung her head. "I can't—I won't—live my life in fear, Sean."

"Well, then, there's a price to pay for that kind of decision. You deserve to know the chances you're taking. You could stay here, at the farm, and flushing out the hit man would be easier—but it would probably take longer."

Susannah turned around and held his searching gaze. Crossing her arms in front of her, she shook her head. "No. If there really is a contract out on me, let's find out. I'd rather get it over with."

Killian understood only too well. "You're courageous," he said, and he meant it.

"No," Susannah told him, her voice quavering, "I'm scared to death. But I miss the kids. I miss teaching."

Killian slowly rose and pushed back his chair. He brought over his now-empty plate and coffee cup. "Okay, Monday you go to work, but I'll be like a shadow, Susannah. Everywhere you go, I go. I'll explain the situation to your principal. He may decide not to let you come back after he knows the potential danger."

"Then I'll stay away," Susannah whispered. "I don't want to endanger my kids. They're innocent."

He set the dishes in the sink and turned to her. Placing his hands on her slumped shoulders, he rasped, "So are you."

Chapter Seven

Uneasy, Killian walked the now-quiet halls of Marshall Elementary School, which was located near the edge of the small town of Glen. All of the children, from grades one through six, were in their classes, the wood-and-glass door to each room closed, and the teachers were busy with their charges. Killian's heart automatically swung back to Susannah, who was happily back at work. The meeting with the principal had gone well. Killian had actually expected him to turn down Susannah's request after hearing about the possibilities.

The principal obviously didn't believe there could be a contract out on Susannah. Nor did she. They didn't want to, Killian thought grimly as he padded quietly down the highly polished floor of an intersecting hall lined with metal lockers.

Dressed in jeans, a tan polo shirt and a light denim jacket that hid his shoulder holster, Killian had a small blueprint layout of the school and its adjacent buildings. He'd already been in Susannah's room and met her ten handicapped students. The children ranged in age from seven to twelve. He hadn't stayed long—he was more interested in the deadly possibilities of his trade.

At lunch, he planned to meet Susannah and her class in the cafeteria. A story had been devised to explain Killian's presence in Susannah's classroom: He was monitoring the course, a teacher from California who was going to set up a similar program out there. Everyone, including the faculty at the morning meeting, had accepted the explanation without reaction. Killian had discovered that Susannah had, from time to time, had teachers from other states come and watch how she conducted her class, because the children had developed more quickly than usual as a result of her unique teaching methods.

The lunch bell rang as Killian finished circling on the map in red ink those areas where a contract killer might hide. Luckily, there weren't many. He missed Susannah's presence, and he hoped to meet her on the way to the cafeteria with her charges.

Susannah's heart sped up at the sight of Killian moving slowly through the hall, which was filled with hundreds of laughing and talking children. She saw his dark eyes lighten as he met and held her gaze, and she smiled, feeling the warmth of his heated look.

Killian moved to the wall of lockers and waited for her.

"Hi," she said breathlessly.

Susannah's eyes shone with a welcome that reached through Killian's heavy armor and touched his heart. An ache began in his chest, an ache that startled Killian. How easily she could touch him with just a look and a soft smile. "How you doing?" Killian fell in step just behind her.

"Fine." Susannah beamed. "It's so good to be back, Sean! I feel like my life's finally coming back together again." Susannah looked tenderly at Freddy, a seven-year-old boy with Down's syndrome who walked at her side, his hand firmly gripping hers. "I really missed my kids," she quavered, looking up at Killian.

Killian had his doubts about Susannah returning to work, about how it might affect her, but he said nothing. Freddy gave her a worshipful look of unqualified love. No wonder Susannah liked working with these special children. They gave fully, in the emotional sense, Killian noted with surprise.

"Are you done with your walk around the school?" Susannah asked as her little flock of children surrounded her. The double doors to the cafeteria were open. She guided her group through them and down the stairs.

"Yeah, I'm done. What can I do to help?"

She smiled and pointed to several long tables with chairs lined up on either side. "See that area?"

"Yes."

"After we get the kids seated, some of the help will bring over their lunches. You go ahead and go through the cafeteria line and meet me over there. I'm going to be pretty busy the next twenty minutes."

Killian sat with his back to the wall. For security reasons, he was glad that the cafeteria was in the basement with no windows. He didn't taste his food—chili, a salad and an apple—or the coffee he'd poured for himself. Instead, he watched Susannah. She wore a bright yellow cotton skirt today, a feminine-looking white short-sleeved blouse, and sandals. Her hair was loose, flowing over her back. She looked beautiful. And it was clear...that there wasn't one child who didn't adore her and positively glow when rewarded with her smile, a touch of her hand, or a brief kiss on the brow.

"Finally!" Susannah sat down with her tray of food. She tucked several stray strands of hair behind her ear and smiled across the table at him.

"You've got your hands full," Killian commented. Lunch was only forty-five minutes long, and Susannah had been up and helping her kids for close to half an hour. Now she'd have to gulp her food down.

"I love it! I wouldn't have it any other way."

Killian quietly suffered the din in the cafeteria, his senses heightened and pummeled at the same time. He nodded to Susannah, but his concentration was on the faculty. There was a possibility that the hit man could pose as a teacher, slip in and try to kill Susannah in the school. All morning he'd been committing faculty faces to memory, his gaze roving restlessly across the huge, noisy cafeteria.

"Well? Did you find what you were looking for?" Susannah asked, eating her chili.

"I located possible sites," Killian said, not wanting to refer directly to the topic for fear of scaring the attentive, listening children who surrounded them. "I'll discuss it with you tonight, when we get home."

With a sigh, Susannah smiled. "Home. It sounds so nice when you say that."

Avoiding her sparkling gaze, which sent a flush of heat sheeting through him, Killian nodded and paid attention to the apple he was eating but not tasting. Home anywhere with Susannah was a dream come true, he decided sourly. Four o'clock couldn't come soon enough because Killian realized he *wanted* time alone with Susannah. Each moment was a precious drop of a dream that, he knew, must someday come to an end. And, like a man lost in the desert, he thirsted for each drop that she gave him simply by being nearby.

"You're exhausted," Killian told Susannah as they worked in the kitchen preparing their dinner. He'd taken on the salad-making duties, and she was frying some steaks.

"Oh, I'm okay. First days are always that way. I'll adjust."

He glanced at her as he cut a tomato deftly with a knife. Susannah had changed into a pair of jeans and a pink sleeveless blouse. She was barefoot. He frowned as he studied her at the stove.

"Maybe you ought to switch to half days for now."

"No... I'll be okay, Sean. It's just that the first days are overwhelming. The children—" she glanced up and met his serious-looking face "—needed reassuring that I wouldn't abandon them. Handicapped children are so sensitized to possible loss of the people they rely on. They live in a very narrow world, and part of their stability is the fixedness of activity within it. If a teacher or a parent suddenly leaves, it's terribly upsetting to them.''

"So you were applying Band-Aids all day?"

She grinned. "You might say that. You look a little tired yourself.''

With a shrug, Killian placed the two salad bowls on the table near their plates. "A little," he lied. He'd hardly slept at all last night.

"Is the school a viable target?" she asked as she arranged their steaks on the plates.

Killian heard the quaver in her voice. He sat down and said, "There are pros and cons to it. The only place where you're really a target is the school-bus loading and unloading zone. The gym facility across the street is two stories tall—ideal for a hit man to hide in and draw a bead on you."

Trying to stay calm, Susannah sat down after pouring them each a cup of coffee. Taking a pink paper napkin, she spread it across her lap. "This is so upsetting, Sean."

"I know.'' The strain on Susannah's face said it all. Killian wished he wasn't always the bearer of such bad tidings.

"It's not your fault.'' She cut a piece of her steak and gave him a sidelong look. "Do these men hit quickly?"

"What do you mean?"

"Well, if a contract's been put out on me, will he try to get it done quickly, instead of waiting months to do it?"

"They like to get paid. They'll do it as quickly as possible to collect the balance of the money."

Susannah pushed some salad around with her fork. "Have you heard from the police about a possible identification from the sketch I gave you a few days ago?"

"Not yet. I was hoping Morgan or the Lexington police would call me. With any luck," Killian said, eating a bite of the succulent steak, "we'll have more answers by tomorrow at the latest."

"And if you find out who my attacker is, you'll be able to know whether or not he's part of a larger drug ring?"

"Yes."

With a sigh, Susannah forced herself to eat. "I just wish it was over."

"So I'd be out of your life."

She gave him a tender look. "You're something good that's happened to me, Sean. I don't want you out of my life."

With a disgruntled look, he growled, "If I were you, I would."

As gently as possible, Susannah broached the subject of Meg with him. "Has your sister had any therapy to help her through the trauma she endured?"

Killian looked up. "A little." He frowned. "Not enough, as far as I'm concerned. Ian, her fiancé, wants to come back into her life, but Meg is afraid to let it happen."

Once again Susannah saw the anguish burning in Killian's eyes, anguish and love for his sister. There was no question but that he cared deeply about her. It was sweet to know that he now trusted her enough to reveal a small piece of his real self. Still, she knew she would have to tread lightly if Sean was to remain open and conversant. What had changed in him to make him more accessible? Possibly today at the school, she thought, cutting another piece of meat.

"Ian still loves her?"

Killian's mouth twisted. "He never stopped."

Susannah moved back to the stove. "You sound confused about that. Why?"

"Because Ian is letting his love for her tear him apart years afterward. He won't forget Meg. He refuses to."

"Love isn't something that dries up and goes away just because there's a tragedy," she said gently, passing him the platter of meat.

Killian placed another piece of steak on his plate, then handed the platter back to Susannah. "If you ask me, love is a special kind of torture. Ian twists in the wind waiting for Meg to take him back."

"He loves her enough to wait," Susannah noted. She saw Killian's eyes harden, the fork suspended halfway to his mouth.

Glancing at her, he snapped, "Love is nothing but pain. I saw it too many times, too many ways, growing up. I've watched Ian suffer. It's not worth it."

"What? Loving someone?" Susannah stopped eating and held his turbulent gaze.

"Yes."

Treading carefully, she asked, "Does Meg allow Ian back into her life in any form?"

"No, only me. She trusts only me."

"Why won't she allow Ian to help her recover?"

Flatly he responded, "Because Meg is disfigured. She's ugly compared to what she used to look like."

Suffering was all too evident on Killian's hard features. Susannah ached for both him and Meg. "She thinks that if Ian sees her he'll leave her anyway?"

"Yes, I guess so. But Ian knows she's no longer beautiful, and he doesn't care. I tried to tell Meg that, but she won't listen."

"Maybe Ian needs to go to Meg directly and confront her about it."

With a snort, Killian shook his head. "Let's put it this way. Our family—what's left of it, Meg and me—are bullheaded."

"She's not being bullheaded," Susannah said softly. "She's sticking her head in the sand and pretending Ian and his feelings don't count."

Killian moved around uncomfortably in his chair. "Sometimes," he muttered defiantly, "running away is the least of all evils."

Susannah met and held his dark blue gaze. "I don't agree. Having the courage to face the other person is always better. You should tell Ian to go to Meg and talk things out."

"If Ian knew where she lived, he'd have done that a long time ago."

She stared at him. "You won't tell him where she lives?"

"How can I? Meg begs me not to. Do you think I'm going to go against her wishes?"

"But," Susannah said lamely, "that would help heal the situation, Sean. Ian wouldn't be left feeling so tortured. Meg wouldn't feel so alone."

Smarting beneath her wisdom, Killian forced his attention back to his plate. He'd lost his appetite. "You're young, Susannah. You're protected. If you'd been kicked around like my family has been, gone through what we've gone through, you wouldn't be so eager for emotional confrontations.''

She felt his panic—and his anger. ''I know I'm naive,'' she whispered.

''Life makes you tired,'' Killian rasped. ''Try getting hit broadside again and again and see how willing you are to get up and confront it again. Believe me, you'll think twice about it. If Ian's smart, he'll get on with his life and forget Meg.''

The depth of his belief in running and hiding frightened Susannah. How many other women had wanted to love Killian? How many had he left? Upset, she could only say, ''If I were Ian, I'd go to Meg. I'd love her enough to find her on my own without your help.''

Killian saw the flash of stubbornness in her eyes, and felt it in her voice. He offered her a twisted, one-cornered smile. ''Idealism doesn't make it in this world, and neither does hope. You've got too much of both, Susannah. All they'll do is hurt you in the end.''

Susannah was getting ready to take a bath around ten that night when the phone rang. Killian was sitting in the living room, reading the newspaper. His head snapped up and his eyes narrowed. Forcing herself to answer the phone, Susannah picked up the receiver.

''Hello?''

''Susannah?''

''Morgan! How are you?''

''I'm fine. Better question is, how are you doing with Killian there?''

She flushed and avoided Killian's interested gaze. "Better," she whispered, suddenly emotional. "Much better."

"Good. Listen, I need to talk to Killian. Can you put him on?"

"Sure. Give Laura and the kids my love, will you?"

"Of course. Are you doing all right physically?"

Susannah heard the guilt in Morgan's voice and knew that he blamed himself in some way for her problems. Her hand tightened on the phone. "I'm improving every day," she promised.

"The headaches?"

Susannah thought for a moment. "Why," she breathed as the realization sank in, "I've had fewer since Killian arrived. Isn't that wonderful?"

"It is."

"I'll put Sean on the phone. Hold on." Susannah held the phone toward Killian. "It's Morgan. He wants to talk to you."

Unwinding from his chair, Killian put the newspaper aside.

Just the touch of Killian's fingers on her own as he took the receiver sent an ache throbbing through Susannah. Sensing that he wanted to be alone to talk to Morgan, Susannah left to take her bath.

Holding the receiver, Killian waited until Susannah was gone. "Morgan?"

"Yes. How's it going?"

"All right," Killian said noncommittally, keeping his voice low. He continued to watch the doorway that Susannah had disappeared through. If the conversation was disturbing, he didn't want her to overhear and become upset. "What's going on?"

"That sketch you sent that Susannah drew?"

"Yes?"

"We've got a positive identification from the FBI. His name is Huey Greaves, and he was a middleman stateside for Santiago's ring. So my hunch was correct—unfortunately. Greaves doubles as a hit man for Santiago whenever another cartel tries to encroach on his territory. The man who was killed was there to pick up drugs that were later found in one of the bus terminal luggage bins. He was from another drug ring— one that's been trying to move in on Santiago's territory."

Killian released a ragged breath, cursing softly. Susannah was in serious danger. "You've given this info to the Lexington police?"

"Yes. They've got an APB out on him. They've also alerted the county sheriff who covers Glen and the Anderson farm."

Grimly Killian gazed around the living room, which was dancing in the shadows created by the two hurricane lamps. "The bastard will hit Susannah."

Morgan sighed. "It's only a matter of time. Santiago—it figures."

"I've got to talk to her about this," Killian rasped. "She's got to know the danger involved. She started teaching today, and under the circumstances I don't think it's a good idea for her to go in tomorrow morning."

"No," Morgan agreed. "We know from experience that Santiago will go to any lengths. His people wouldn't care if there are children involved. Keep her at the farm, Killian. It's safer for everyone that way."

Killian almost laughed at the irony of the situation. No place was safe for Susannah—not even with him. "Yeah, I'll keep her here."

"You know Glen doesn't have much of a police department. The county sheriff is the only one who can help you if you get into trouble. Get the number and keep it handy. With budget cuts, they only have two patrol cars for the entire county, so don't expect too much. A two-hour delay wouldn't be unusual, Killian. I'm afraid you're really on your own on this one. The county sheriff knows who you are and why you're there, and if they see this guy they'll call to let you know—and send a sheriff's cruiser in your direction as soon as humanly possible."

"Good." At least the police and the FBI were working together on this. Still, chances were that when the hit went down it would be Killian against the killer.

"Stay in touch," Morgan said.

"Thanks, Morgan. I will." Killian scowled as he hung up the phone. He wasn't looking forward to telling Susannah the bad news.

Susannah couldn't sleep. She was restless, tossing and turning on her ancient brass bed. The night air was warm, and she pushed off the sheet. Her watch read 2:00 a.m. It was the phone call from Morgan that had left her sleepless.

With a muffled sound of frustration, Susannah got up. She didn't want to wake Sean. Just the thought of him sent a flurry of need through her as she padded softly down the hall to the kitchen. Perhaps a cup of hot chamomile tea would help settle her screaming nerves so that she could sleep. But, she warned herself, tea wasn't going to stop the simmering desire that had been building in her for days.

Susannah ran a hand through her unbound hair, then opened the cabinet and took out a cup and saucer. Killian had warned her away from him—told her that he was no good for her. Why couldn't she listen to his thinly veiled threat?

"Susannah?"

Gasping, she whirled around, nearly dropping the cup from her hand. Killian stood in the doorway, his drawstring pajamas barely held up by his narrow hips. His eyes were soft with sleep, and his hair was tangled across his brow. Her heart pounding, Susannah released a breath.

"You scared me."

"Sorry," he muttered, any remaining sleepiness torn from him as he studied her in the shadowy moonlight that crossed the kitchen. Her knee-length white gown gave her an angelic look, and the moonlight outlined her body like a lover's caress through the light cotton fabric. The dark frame of hair emphasized the delicateness of her features, especially her parted lips.

"I—I couldn't sleep." She gestured toward the kettle on the stove. "I thought I'd make some chamomile tea."

"Morgan's call upset you?"

"Yes."

Easing into the room, Killian crossed to the table and sat down. His head was screaming at him to go back to bed, but his heart clamored for her closeness.

"Make me a cup, will you?"

"Sure." Susannah's pulse wouldn't seem to settle down, and she busied herself at the counter, attempting to quell her nervousness. Killian's body was hard and lean. She wondered what it would be like to kiss him, to feel his arms around her.

As Susannah turned, the cups of tea in her hands, the window at the kitchen counter shattered, glass exploding in all directions.

"Get down!" Killian shouted. Launching himself out of his chair, he took Susannah with him as he slammed to the floor. More glass shattered, splintering in rainbow fragments all around them.

Susannah groaned under Killian's weight, her mind spinning with shock. She could hear Killian's harsh breathing, and his cursing, soft and strained. Almost instantly she felt his steely grip on her arms as he dragged her upward and positioned her against the corner cabinets for protection.

Her eyes wide, she took in the harshness in his sweaty features.

"The hit man," he rasped. *Dammit!* He'd left his pistol in the bedroom. He noticed small, bloody cuts on Susannah's right arm.

"But—how?"

Killian shook his head, putting his finger to his lips. Silence was crucial right now. The hit man had to be on the porch. But why the hell hadn't he heard him? Felt him? A hundred questions battered Killian. His senses were now screamingly alert. He had to get to his gun, or they were both dead!

Gripping Susannah's wrist, Killian tugged and motioned for her to follow him. If they couldn't make it to his bedroom, they were finished. The last thing he wanted was Susannah dead. The thought spurred him into action.

Gasping for breath, Susannah scrambled out of the kitchen on her hands and knees. In the darkened hall, Killian jerked her to her feet, shoving her forward and into his room. Instantly he pushed her onto the floor and motioned for her to wriggle beneath the bed and remain there.

Killian's fingers closed over the pistol on the nightstand. The feel of the cool metal was reassuring. Now they had a chance. His eyes narrowed as he studied the window near his bed and the open door to his room.

"Stay down!" he hissed. "Whatever happens, stay here!"

Tears jammed into Susannah's eyes as she looked up into his taut, glistening features. Here was the mercenary. The soldier who could kill. She opened her mouth, then snapped it shut.

"Don't move!" Killian warned. He leaped lightly to his feet, every muscle in his body tense with anticipation. He tugged at the blanket so that it hung off the bed and concealed Susannah's glaringly white nightgown. Swiftly he turned on his heel and moved to the door, his hands wrapped around the pistol that he held high and at the ready.

Killian was angry at himself—angry that he'd dropped his guard because he cared for Susannah. He pressed himself hard against the wall and listened. His nostrils flared to catch any unusual scent. Morgan Trayhern had called him a hound from hell on more than one occasion because of his acutely honed senses. Well, they'd saved his life more than once. Tonight, he had to count on his abilities to save Susannah.

As he ducked out of the entrance and quickly looked up and down the hall, Killian saw no evidence of the hit man. Then a creak of wood made him freeze. There! The kitchen! His heart was a thudding sledgehammer in his chest, his quiet breathing was ragged. The bastard was in the kitchen.

There! Killian heard the crunch of glass. How close to the kitchen doorway was he? He continued down the hall soundlessly, on the balls of his feet. His hands sweaty, beads of perspiration running down his temples, Killian focused like a laser on his quarry. Susannah's killer. Only two more feet and he'd have enough of an angle to peer into the darkened depths of the kitchen. Every muscle in his body stiffened with expectation.

Another crunch of glass. The sound was directional, giving away where the hit man stood. Instantly Killian launched himself forward, flattening himself against the hardwood floor, both hands in front of him, the snout of the Beretta aimed. Seeing the darkened shape of a man move, he squeezed off two shots. The sounds reverberated through the farmhouse. Damn! He'd missed!

The hit man fired back, a silencer on his gun cloaking the sound to light pops. Killian rolled to the left, the door jamb his shield. Wood cracked and splintered as bullets savagely tore at the barrier. His mind working rapidly, Killian counted off the shots. Six. More than likely the bastard had nine bullets in his clip. Then he'd have to reload.

The scrambling over glass continued. Killian kept low. He realized with terror that the bedroom where Susannah was hiding was directly behind the hit man. If Killian fired, his shots could go through the walls and hit her. Damn!

Breathing hard, his lips pulled away from clenched teeth, Killian grabbed a piece of wood near his bare feet, and threw it into the kitchen.

Two more shots were fired at it in quick succession.

Good! Only one more round before he'd have to take precious seconds to reload. Stinging sweat dripped into his eyes, and he blinked it away.

In those seconds, waiting for the hit man to make his move, Killian realized that he loved Susannah. Where had such a crazy idea come from? Tightening his grip on the Beretta, he rose onto one knee, ready to fire.

An explosion of movement occurred in the kitchen. Before Killian could fire, the table was tipped over, slamming against the doorway and spoiling his shot. The screen door was ripped off its hinges as a dark figure scrambled out. The thudding of running feet filled the air.

Cursing roundly, Killian leaped over the table. The son of a bitch! Sprinting onto the porch, Killian saw the hit man fleeing toward the road, where his car must be hidden. Digging his toes into the soft, wet grass, Killian started after him. The direction the hit man was running was in line with the Andersons' farmhouse, not more than a quarter mile away. Killian couldn't risk a stray bullet hitting the house or its occupants.

Running hard, he cut through the orchard. Ahead, he saw a dark blue car. The hit man jerked the door open, disappeared inside and hit the accelerator.

The nondescript car leaped forward, dirt and clods flying up, leaving a screen of dust in its wake. Killian memorized the license plate number before the car was swallowed up by the darkness. Lowering his pistol, he continued to run toward the Anderson residence. He wanted to report the car's license number to the sheriff and call Morgan. More than likely the vehicle was a rental car, and the hit man had signed for it with an alias at an airport—probably Lexington.

Killian's mind spun with options, with necessary procedures that would have to be instituted quickly.

Reaching the house, he wasn't surprised to find the Andersons still asleep, completely unaware of what had just occurred. Susannah's house was nearly a half mile away with plenty of orchard to absorb the sounds of battle.

Breathing hard, Killian entered the house via the kitchen and found the phone there on the wall. Setting his gun nearby on the counter, he shakily dialed the county sheriff. As he waited for someone to answer, his heart revolved back to Susannah. Was she all right? He recalled the cuts to her right arm, caused by the shattering glass. Anger with himself because he hadn't protected her as well as he should have filled Killian. As soon as he'd reported the incident, he'd get back to the house and care for Susannah.

Lying on her belly, Susannah had no idea how long she remained frozen. Her heart was beating hard, and her fingers were dug into the wooden floor. Sean! Was he all right? What had happened? Did she dare risk coming out from beneath the bed to find out? There had been no sound for about fifteen minutes. Her mind was playing tricks on her. Maybe Sean was bleeding to death on the kitchen floor and she didn't know it. Should she move from her hiding place? Should she stay?

She closed her eyes as tears leaked into them. Sean couldn't be dead! He just couldn't! The attack had ripped away her doubts. She loved Killian. It was that simple—and that complicated. Lying there, shaking badly as the adrenaline began to seep out of her bloodstream, she pressed her brow against her hands. Sean had ordered her not to move—no matter what. But how could she remain here? If he was lying wounded somewhere, how could she not move?

With a little cry, Susannah made her decision.

"Susannah?"

Killian! She gasped as he pulled the blanket away. Her eyes widened enormously as he got down on his hands and knees.

"Sean?"

He smiled grimly and reached for her. "Yeah. I'm all right, colleen. Everything's okay. The hit man got away. Come on, crawl out of there."

Susannah discovered how wobbly she was as she got to her feet. Killian gripped her hands.

"I—I don't think I can stand," she quavered, looking up into his dark, sweaty features.

"I'm not too steady myself," he answered with a rasp. He drew Susannah into his arms and brought her against him. The contact with her was shocking. Melting. Killian groaned as she leaned heavily against him, her arms around him, her head against his shoulder.

"Sweet," he whispered, holding her tightly—holding her so hard he was afraid he was going to crush her. The natural scent of her—a fragrant smell, like lilacs—encircled his nostrils. Killian dragged in that scent, life after the odors of death. He felt Susannah shift and lift her head. Without thinking, he cupped her chin and guided her lips to his mouth.

The meeting was fiery, purging. He felt the softness of her lips, felt them flow open, their heat, their moistness overwhelming his heightened senses. Time ceased to exist. All he was aware of, all he wanted, was her. The warmth of Susannah's breasts pressing softly against his chest, her softness against his hardness, shattered the last of his control.

He groaned, taking her mouth hungrily, sliding against her, absorbing her warmth, her womanliness. His breathing grew chaotic, fevered, as she returned his inflammatory kiss. His fingers sliding into her hair, Killian gripped the silky strands, framing her face, holding her captive as he absorbed her into him like a starving man.

Susannah moaned, but it was a moan of utter surrender mingled with pleasure. She found herself pressed onto the bed, with Killian's tense body against her, driving her into the mattress. The near brush with death—the fear of losing him—overwhelmed her, and she sought blindly to reassure herself that she was alive, that he was safe. There was security in Sean's arms, those powerful bands that trapped her, holding her captive beneath him. With a fierce need, she returned his searching kiss.

"I need you, I need you," Killian rasped against her wet, soft mouth. "Now. I need you now...." He felt her arch beneath him, giving him the answer he sought. He'd nearly lost Susannah to an assailant's bullet. The warmth of her flesh, the eagerness of her beneath him, could have been destroyed in a split second. Sliding his shaky hands beneath her rumpled gown, he sought and found her slender rib cage, then moved upward. The instant his hands curved around her small breasts, he heard her cry out. But it was a cry of utter pleasure, not fear or pain. The husky sound coming from her throat increased the heat in his lower body. Never had he wanted a woman more. Never had he loved a woman as he loved Susannah.

The fierceness of his roiling emotions shattered Killian's ironclad control. He was helpless beneath her hands. They were gliding over his taut back and shoulders as he pulled the gown off her. In moments his pajamas were in a heap on the wooden floor. Her fingers dug convulsively into his bunched shoulders as he leaned down and captured the tight peak of her nipple with his insistent lips. She became wild, untamed, beneath him, moving her head from side to side, begging him to enter her.

The fever in his blood tripled, sang through him as he felt her thighs open to welcome him. He wanted to take it slow, to make it good for Susannah, but the fiery blood beating through him ripped away all but his primal need to plunge deep into her—to bury himself in her life, escaping the death that had stalked them less than an hour earlier.

Framing her face with his hands, Killian looked down into her dazed, lustrous eyes as he moved forward to meet her. He wanted to imprint Susannah's lovely features on his heart and mind forever. The moment he entered her hot, womanly confines, a low, vibrating growl ripped out of him. He couldn't stop his forward plunge—didn't want to. His need for this feverish coupling was like a storm that had waited too long to expend itself.

Killian's fingers tightened against Susannah's face and he stiffened as liquid fire encircled him, captured him, leaving him mindless, aware of nothing but a rainbow of sensations, each more powerful, more overwhelming, than the next. When Susannah moved her hips, drawing him even deeper inside her, he sucked in a ragged breath. Never had he experienced heaven like this. He leaned down, savoring her lips, drowning in the splendor of her sweet, fiery offering.

Then nothing existed but the touching and sliding of their bodies against each other, satin against steel. Susannah was soft, giving, bending to Killian's needs with a sweet suppleness. He was hard, demanding— plunging and taking. Her lilac fragrance surrounded him as he buried his face in the silky folds of her hair. In moments, an explosive feeling enveloped him, freezing him into an immobility of such intense plea- sure that he could only gasp in response. As she moved her hips sinuously against him, he could no more control himself than a rain storm could hold back from spending itself on the lush warmth of the earth.

Afterward, moments glided and fused together as Killian lay spent. He raised his head and realized that his fingers were still tightly grasping the thick strands of Susannah's hair, as if he were afraid she'd slip away from him—as if this were one of his fevered dreams, ready to flee when he opened his eyes. Susannah's lashes fluttered upward, and he held his breath, drowning in the glorious gray of her eyes.

The soft, trembling smile that curved her lips sent another sheet of heat through Killian. He felt her hot, wet tightness still around him, holding him, and he groaned.

"I feel like I've gone to heaven," he rasped against her lips. And then he added weakly, "Or as close as I'll ever get to heaven, because I'm bound for hell."

"You *are* heaven," Susannah managed huskily, held captive by him in all ways, luxuriating in his strength and masculinity.

Carefully Killian untangled his hand from her hair and touched her swollen lips. With a grimace, he whispered, "I'm sorry, colleen, I got carried away. I didn't mean to hurt you."

Susannah kissed his scarred fingers. "I'm fine. How could you hurt me?"

He shakily traced her smooth forehead and the arch of her eyebrow. "In a million ways," he assured her.

With a tender smile, Susannah framed his damp features. No longer was the man with the hard face staring down at her. No, this was the very human, vulnerable side of Sean Killian. And she reveled fiercely in his being able to shed his outer shell—to give himself to her in an even more important, wonderful way.

Gently Killian moved aside and brought Susannah into his arms as he lay on the bed. "Come here," he whispered, holding her tight for a long, long time. The moments ran together for him. Susannah's arm flowed across his chest, and one of her long, lovely legs lay across his own. He blinked his eyes several times, trying to think coherently. It was nearly impossible with Susannah in his arms.

"You're all a man could ever dream of having," he told her in a low, unsteady voice as he kissed her cheek, and then her awaiting lips. Lying there with her in his arms, he caressed her cheek.

Susannah melted within his embrace, savoring the feel of his fingers moving lightly across her shoulder, down her arm to her hip. He was stroking her as if she were a purring cat. And wasn't she? "I'll never be sorry this happened," she admitted breathlessly. "Never."

As Killian lay there, his mind finally beginning to take over from the lavalike emotions that had exploded in a volcano lain dormant too long, he tasted bitterness in his mouth. There was Susannah, innocent and trusting in his arms, her eyes shining with such adoration that it made him sick inside. She didn't know his sordid past, didn't know the ghosts that still haunted him.

"I shouldn't have done this to you," he rasped, frowning. Yet he couldn't stop touching her, sliding his hands across her satiny flesh and feeling her effortless response.

"No!" Susannah forced herself up onto one elbow. She reached out, her hand on his chest, where his heart lay. "We both wanted this, Sean. *Both* of us."

He grimaced. "It shouldn't have happened," he said, more harshly.

"Really?" Susannah couldn't keep the sarcasm out of her tone, and she was sorry for it.

Unable to meet her eyes, he shook his head and threw the covers aside. "I was to protect you, Susannah!"

"Loving someone isn't protecting them?"

He glanced at her sharply as he forced himself to get up and leave her side. If he stayed, he'd want to love her all over again, with the fierceness of a breaking thunderstorm.

"I was paid to protect you, dammit!" he flared, moving around the bed and going to the dresser. Jerking open the drawer, he retrieved jeans and a polo shirt.

Sitting up in bed, Susannah suddenly felt bereft. Abandoned. Quiet tension thrummed through the room, and a chill washed over her. Killian put on boxer shorts and the jeans. His face was hard again, his mouth set in a thin line.

"Sean, what's going on? I liked what we shared. I like you. Why are you so angry and upset about it?"

"You'd better get cleaned up, Susannah," he told her tautly, pulling the shirt over his head. "Take a shower and get dressed. The sheriff is sending out a cruiser to check out what happened with the hit man. He'll probably be here in a half hour or so."

Forcing herself to her feet, Susannah moved over to him. His movements were abrupt and tense. She gripped his arm.

"The police can wait," she said hoarsely, searching his dark, unfathomable eyes. "*We* can't."

Her fingers were like small, exquisite brands burning into his flesh. Killian pulled away from Susannah. "There is no 'we'!" he said harshly. It was pure, unadulterated hell looking down at her standing there naked and beautiful before him. "Look at you! Even now you can't protect yourself against the likes of someone like me. It shouldn't have happened, Susannah! It was my fault. I wanted—needed you so damned bad I could taste it." Aggravated, Killian ran his fingers through his mussed hair. "I broke a cardinal rule that I've never broken before—I got involved with the person I was supposed to protect." He gave her a sad look, his voice cracking with emotion. "I'm sorry. I'm sorry it happened. You didn't deserve this on top of everything else, Susannah."

Chapter Eight

Susannah had barely stepped out of the shower when the sheriff's cruiser arrived. Going to her bedroom, she dressed in a sensible pair of dark green cotton slacks and a white short-sleeved blouse. Her hair was still damp, and she braided the strands together, fastening the ends with a rubber band. Her hands shook as she put on white socks and a pair of sneakers.

The terror of nearly being killed warred with Sean's reaction to their lovemaking, buffeting her weary senses. Each time she replayed the conversation, it made no sense to her. Why was he sorry he'd loved her? She wasn't. Touching her bangs with trembling fingers, she took one look in the mirror. Her face was pale, and her eyes were dark and huge. And her lips... Susannah groaned softly. Her mouth looked wonderfully ravished, slightly swollen and well kissed.

Entering the kitchen, Susannah saw the damage from the gunfire for the first time. Killian had set the table upright, and he and the two deputies sat at the table, their faces grim. Across the wooden floor, glass lay splintered and glinting in the lamplight.

Killian glanced up. Susannah stood poised just inside the room. He was struck by her beauty, her simple clothing—the luster in her gray eyes that he knew was meant for him alone. Trying to steel himself against his still-turbulent emotions, he got up.

"Come over here and sit down," he invited, his voice rough. "They've caught the guy who tried to kill us."

Gasping in surprise, Susannah came forward. "They did?"

"Yes, ma'am," a large, beefy deputy volunteered. "Thanks to Mr. Killian's quick reporting, we got him just as he was trying to leave the Glen town limits."

Killian pulled the chair out for her so that she could sit down. It hardly seemed possible, but Susannah looked even paler.

"You want some coffee?" he asked. Dammit, why did he have to sound so harsh with her? He was angry with himself, with his lack of control. It was he who had initiated their lovemaking.

"Please." Susannah tried to ignore Killian's overwhelming male presence—to concentrate on the deputy, whose name tag read Birch. But it was impossible. "Deputy Birch, what can you tell us about this hit man?" she managed to say, her voice unsteady.

"Not much. We're putting him through the paces right now back at the station. I do know he'll get put in jail without bail. The judge won't hear his case until nine this morning."

Susannah looked at the wall clock. It was 3:00 a.m., yet she felt screamingly awake. Was this how Sean felt all the time? Did a mercenary ever relax? As Killian moved around the counter, which was strewn with wood and glass debris, Susannah sensed an explosiveness around him.

"How may I help?" Susannah asked the deputies in a low, off-key voice.

"Just give us your statement, Miss Anderson." Birch threw a look at Killian. "I'd say your guardian angel here saved you."

She forced a smile that she didn't feel. "Yes, well, Mr. Killian is protective, if nothing else." Susannah saw him twist a look across his shoulder at her. His eyes were dark and angry. What had she done to deserve his anger? She hoped against hope that, when the deputies left, she and Sean could sit and talk this out.

Killian moved restlessly around the kitchen. It was 4:00 a.m., and the deputies were wrapping up their investigation. Susannah was looking exhausted, her adrenaline high clearly worn off, a bruised-looking darkness beneath her eyes.

"We'll be in touch shortly," Birch promised as the deputies stood up and ended their visit.

"Thank you," Susannah told them wearily, meaning it. She watched as Killian escorted the officers out to the porch, where they talked in low voices she couldn't overhear. Exhausted, she stood up, feeling as if she'd gone days without sleep. As much as she wanted to wait for Sean to return, to discuss whatever problem had sprung up between them, Susannah knew she didn't have the emotional strength for the confrontation. It would have to wait.

In her room, Susannah set the alarm for seven, so that she could call the principal and tell him she wouldn't be able to teach today. She lay down on the bed, not caring that she was still dressed, and fell asleep immediately. In her dreams, Killian loved her with his primal hunger all over again.

Susannah awoke with a start, her heart pounding. Sunlight was pouring in through the curtains at a high angle. What time was it? Groggily she looked at her watch. It was noon! She barely recalled getting up at seven to make the call and going straight back to bed.

Sitting for a moment, she allowed herself time to get reoriented. Had last night been some terrible combination of nightmare and dream? Killian's words about heaven and hell came back to her. That was what last night had been for her: tasting both extremes. It had been heaven loving Sean, feeling the intensity of his need for her. The hell had arrived earlier, in the form of a killer who'd wanted to take her life. Rubbing her brow, Susannah felt the beginnings of a headache. A heartache would be more appropriate. Why was Sean sorry he'd loved her?

When Susannah went to the kitchen, she found it almost as good as new. The only thing missing was the window over the sink. The floor had been swept clean of debris and mopped, the counters cleared of any evidence of the violent episode. She looked around. The splintered wood in the doorway had been removed. Either Killian or her father was busy making repairs.

What couldn't be repaired as quickly were the bullet holes along the kitchen wall. They were an ugly reminder, and Susannah stood there, rubbing her arms absently, feeling very cold.

"It's almost like new."

Gasping, Susannah turned at the sound of Killian's low voice. He stood at the screen door, a piece of wood in his hand. "You scared me to death!" She placed her hand against her pounding heart.

Entering, Killian scowled. Susannah looked sleepy, her eyes puffy, and her mouth— He groaned inwardly. Her mouth looked beautifully pouty, the force of his kisses last night still stamped there. The ache to kiss her all over again, to ease the fear lingering in her eyes by taking her into his arms, flowed through him. Savagely he destroyed the feeling.

"Sorry," he muttered. "I didn't mean to scare you." He stalked across the kitchen and placed the wood against the door jamb. It fit perfectly. Now all he had to do was nail it into place.

"That's okay," she reassured him, a little breathlessly, "I'm just jumpy right now."

"Now you know how a mercenary feels twenty-four hours a day." He gave her a cheerless look. Killian wanted to convey in every way possible the miserable life he led—no place for a decent human being like Susannah. He wished she'd quit looking at him like that, with that innocence that drove him crazy with need.

Forcing herself to move, Susannah poured herself some fresh coffee. "Has the sheriff called yet?"

"Yes. Greaves was the man. The same one that nearly killed you at the bus station. He isn't talking, but I spoke to Morgan earlier, and he's working with the sheriff. The FBI are still in on it, too." Killian placed the board against the wall and went to the icebox. He wasn't hungry, but he knew he had to eat.

Biting down on her lower lip, Susannah glanced over at Killian as he brought out whole wheat bread, lunch meat and mustard. "Is it over, then?"

"I don't know. Morgan is sending a message through a third party to Santiago's cartel in Peru. He's ordering him to lift the contract on you or we'll start extradition procedures against more of the cartel honchos."

"What makes you think they'll lift the contract?" Susannah watched him slap some mustard on the bread and top it with several pieces of lunch meat. His features were unreadable, as usual. What was he feeling? Hadn't their loving meant anything to him? He was acting as if it had never happened!

Killian moved to the table and sat down with his sandwich. "This particular drug family is in plenty of hot water already with the Peruvian government, so they don't need any more attention from the authorities. Besides, Greaves is one of their top men who does dirty work for them in this country. They don't want to risk him spilling the beans to the American authorities on what he knows about the drug shipments to the U.S. He's been in a position to know about a lot of things. No, they'll probably make the deal and take the heat off you."

Turning around so that her back rested against the counter, Susannah crossed her arms. Killian sat, frowning darkly while he munched on the sandwich. "How soon will we know?" she asked softly.

"Morgan says a day or two at the latest. He'll call us."

Her arms tightened against herself. "And if they agree to lift the contract, what will you do?"

Forcing himself to meet her gaze, Killian growled, "I'll leave."

The words plunged into her heart like a dagger. Susannah felt as if someone had just gutted her. Turning away, she realized she was out of sorts, still waking up, in no mental—or emotional—state to discuss last night. Killian was biting into his sandwich as if he were angry with it. His blue eyes were turbulent, and he was markedly restless. Misery avalanched Susannah.

"I'm going into town," Killian said abruptly, rising. He'd choked down the sandwich, not tasting it at all, and now it sat like a huge rock in his stomach. The suffering on Susannah's face was real, and he had no control over his response to it. He'd made her this way with one lousy indiscretion—with his selfish need of her. Killian stalked to the screen door, which he'd recently rehung with new hinges.

"I've got to pick up the new glass for that window. I'll be back later."

Hurt, Susannah nodded. When Killian had left, she remained where she was, her head bowed, her eyes shut. Forcing back tears, she realized that even though he'd made wild, passionate love to her this morning, it had been little more than that. She knew nothing of the mercenary type of man. Was this part of their pattern—loving a woman and then leaving her? Susannah laughed derisively as she opened her eyes.

There were a lot of men out there like that, unwilling to commit to a real, ongoing relationship, so they used women, then left them. Was Killian like that?

Her heart cried no, but as Susannah moved around the kitchen, she couldn't come up with a more reasonable answer. Still, Killian just didn't seem the type not to be loyal. Perhaps, when he came back with the window this afternoon, both of them would be more settled after the frightening events of last night, and she could talk to him.

Killian stood back, pleased with the new window gracing the kitchen. He was wildly aware that Susannah was nearby. She'd taken care of the bullet holes, filling them with spackling compound. In a day or two, when they'd dried sufficiently, she would sandpaper them smooth and paint over them. No one would realize the bullet holes were there—no one except them. Some things, he thought with disgust, one never forgot.

As Killian poured himself some coffee and went to sit on the front porch swing, he knew he'd never forget loving Susannah. The swing creaked beneath his weight, the gentle back-and-forth motion taking the edge off his screamingly taut nerves and aching heart. Taking a sip of the hot, black liquid, he narrowed his eyes, seeing nothing in front of him. He loved Susannah. How had it happened? When? He shook his head as a powerful sadness moved through him.

It didn't matter. No woman had ever captured his imagination, his feelings, the closely guarded part of him that still knew how to dream, as she had. More than anything, he wanted to spend the whole day loving her, falling asleep with her supple warmth beside him—waking up to love her all over again. But this time he wanted to move slowly, to savor Susannah, to pleasure her. He doubted she'd gotten much pleasure the first time. He'd stolen from her like a thief, because he'd needed her so badly, he thought sourly.

Reality drenched Killian as he swung slowly back and forth. Susannah could never know how he loved her.

"Sean?"

He snapped his head up. Susannah stood uncertainly at the screen door.

"Yes?" He heard the brittleness in his voice and automatically steeled himself.

"I need to talk with you," Susannah said, and pushed the screen door open. "I was waiting for you to take a break."

His mouth thinning, he picked up his now-empty coffee cup in both hands. If he didn't, he would reach for Susannah, who had come to lean against the porch railing, near the swing.

"The window's in."

Susannah nodded, licking her dry lips. "Yes... It looks good as new." She shrugged. "I wish... I wish we could fix ourselves like that window—be brand-new all over again and not have a memory of what happened last night."

"That's what makes us human, I guess," he answered gruffly. The terrible suffering in Susannah's eyes was beginning to tear him apart.

Susannah nervously clasped her hands in front of her and forced herself to look at Killian. His face was closed and unreadable, his blue eyes narrowed and calculating. "We've got to talk," Susannah began hoarsely. "I can't go on like this."

"Like what?"

Taking in a ragged breath, Susannah whispered, "We loved each other last night, Sean. Doesn't that mean anything to you?"

Wincing inwardly, Killian saw tears forming in her eyes. His mouth going dry, a lump growing in his throat, he rasped, "Dammit, Susannah, it shouldn't have happened!"

"I'm not sorry, Sean, if that's what you're worried about."

He gave her a dark look. "Well, I am. We didn't use protection. For all I know, you could be pregnant."

Startled, Susannah allowed his growling words to sink in. "Is that what's bothering you? That I might be pregnant?"

With a disgusted sound, Killian lunged to his feet, tense. "Doesn't it worry you?" he snapped. Desperate for anything that might force her to understand that there was no possible future for them, he zeroed in on that argument.

Susannah cringed beneath his taunting words. It felt as if Killian could explode at any moment. He stood next to her, tense and demanding. "Well—"

"I didn't think you were looking ahead," he rasped.

"That isn't the issue," Susannah said, forcing herself to hold his angry gaze. "The real issue is whether or not we have something special, something worth pursuing—together."

No one loved her courage more than he did. For the first time, Killian saw the stubborn jut of her jaw and the defiance in her eyes. He told himself he shouldn't be surprised by Susannah's hidden strength.

With a hiss, he turned away. "There is no us!"

"Why? Why can't there be?"

Killian whirled on her, his breathing ragged. "Because there can't be, Susannah!" He glared at her. "There will be no relationship between us." It tormented him to add, "You got that?"

Her lips parting, Susannah took a step away from Killian. Although his face was implacable, his eyes gave him away. Her womanly intuition told her that at least part of what he was saying was bluff.

"What are you afraid of?" she said, her voice quavering.

Stunned by her insight, Killian backed away. "Nothing!" he lied. His chest heaving with inner pain—and the pain he was causing Susannah—he added savagely, "Stick with your dreams and hopes, Susannah. I don't belong in your idealistic world. I can't fit into it. I never will." His voice deepened with anguish. "I warned you to stay away from me. I warned you that it wouldn't be any good if you got close to me."

Rattled, Susannah whispered, "But I did! And I don't regret it, Sean. Doesn't that make any difference?"

Killian shook his head, his voice cracking. "Listen to me. I told you, I'm out of your life. I'm here for maybe a day or two more at the most. I'm sorry I made love to you. I had no right. It was my fault." He gave a helpless wave of his arm.

Her eyes rounded. How callous, how cold, he sounded. "I don't believe you mean that," she said, her voice beginning to shake with real anger.

He stared at her, openmouthed. "Don't look at me like that, Susannah. I'm no knight on a white horse."

Hurting, fighting not to cry in front of him, Susannah stared up at him. "What man is?" she cried. "We're all human beings, with strengths and weaknesses. You try to keep people at arm's length by making them think you're cold and cruel. I know you're not! You're bluffing, Sean."

Startled, Killian felt panic as never before. But he loved Susannah enough to allow her the freedom she didn't want from him. If only he could explain it to her... Moving forward, he gripped her arm with just enough force to let her know he meant what he was going to say. "Bluffing? When I leave and you don't hear from me again, that's no bluff, Susannah. I'm sorry I ever met you, because I've hurt you, and I never meant to do that. I swear I didn't." He gave her a little shake. When he spoke again, there was desperation in his voice. "Move on with your life after I leave. Find a good man here—someone who believes in dreams like you do. I've told you before—I'm bound for hell. Well, I got a little taste of heaven with you. It was damned good, Susannah. I'll never forget it, but I'm a realist." He released her and stepped back.

With a little sob, Susannah lifted her hand and pressed it against her mouth. Giving her a hopeless look, Killian spun on his heel and stalked back into the farmhouse.

Swaying, Susannah caught herself and sat down heavily in the swing, afraid her knees would give out entirely. Killian's words pummeled her, cut through her. She felt flayed by his anger. Hell was here, right now. It took a long minute for Susannah to wrestle with her unraveling emotions and force herself not to end up in a weeping heap. Miserably, she wiped the moisture from her eyes. In two days or less, they would know from Morgan whether or not the drug cartel would agree to the deal. If they did, Killian was out of her life in an instant. He wanted to run. He wanted to escape.

Killian slowly finished packing his bag. Morgan had just called to let him know the Peruvian cartel had agreed to lift the contract on Susannah. At least now she would be safe. His hand tightened around the handle of his satchel. The badly beaten leather bag had seen better days—like him, he thought wearily.

Right now, Susannah was out in the garden, barefoot, wearing her old straw hat, doing the weeding. Two of the most miserable days of Killian's life had somehow managed to pass. Never had he suffered so much, known agony as devastating as this. Every fiber of his being wanted to go out and say goodbye to Susannah. He hesitated, torn. If he did, he knew there was a good possibility he couldn't continue his charade. Last night, he'd heard Susannah sobbing softly, as if she were trying to hide her pain by crying into her pillow.

Tears jammed into Killian's eyes. With a disgusted sound, he forced them back. No, he didn't dare say goodbye to Susannah in person.

"Dammit," he rasped, his voice cracking. He scribbled a quick note, then went into the kitchen and left it on the table where Susannah would see it. He took one last look around the old, dilapidated farmhouse. Capturing the memories, he stored and locked them in the vault of his scarred heart.

Taking one last look toward the garden area, Killian saw Susannah down on her hands and knees, still weeding. Dragging in a deep, painful breath, Killian silently whirled around and left. Forever.

Susannah washed most of the dirt from her hands with water from the hose outside the garden fence. It was nearly four, and she knew she had to prepare supper. Where was Sean? She'd hardly seen him in the past two days. And why hadn't Morgan called? It hurt to think. It hurt to feel, Susannah thought as she slipped the straw hat off her head and entered the kitchen.

Almost immediately, she saw the note on the table. Next to it was a glass containing a freshly cut yellow rose. Frowning, her heart doing a funny skipping beat, Susannah went over to the table. Sitting down, she shakily unfolded the note.

Dear Susannah:
Morgan called about an hour ago to tell me that the drug cartel has promised to leave you alone. You're safe, and that's what is important.

By the time you get this note, I'll be gone. I'm sorry I couldn't say goodbye. Being with you was heaven, Susannah. And for a man bound for hell, it was too much to take. Cowardice comes in many forms, and I didn't have the courage to say goodbye to you. You deserve better than me, as I've told you many times before.

You were a rainbow in my life. I never thought someone like me would ever see one, much less meet one in the form of a woman. You deserve only the best, Susannah. I'm not a man who prays much, but I will pray for your happiness. God knows, you deserve it. Killian.

A sob lodged in Susannah's throat. She stared at the paper, the words blurring as tears rose then spilled out of her eyes and down her cheeks. She gripped the letter hard, reading it and rereading it. There were so many mixed messages. It hadn't been the hardened mercenary writing this. No, it had been the very human, hurting man beneath his warrior's facade.

Crying softly, Susannah put the note aside and buried her face in her hands. The school had given her another month's leave to recover from the shooting incident. Lifting her head, she wiped the tears from her eyes. She had a month.... Gathering her strewn emotions, Susannah decided to call Morgan and talk to him about Sean. Outwardly, Killian was behaving like a bastard, but a bastard wouldn't have written about her being a rainbow in his life.

Susannah worked to compose herself. She'd gone through so much in such a short amount of time. A huge part of her didn't believe Sean's letter. Never had she felt this way toward a man. She'd been "in love" before, but that relationship hadn't matured. No man had made her feel so vibrant or so alive. Did she even know what real love was? Had Sean touched her heart with genuine love? Susannah didn't know, but one way or another she intended to find out.

She brought the glass containing the yellow rose forward. Touching the delicate petals with her fingers, the fragrance encircling her, Susannah realized that Killian might be tough in many ways, but, like this rose that he'd symbolically left her, he had a vulnerable, fragile underside.

That realization gave Susannah hope as nothing else could have. She'd call Morgan and begin an investigation into Sean and the world he called hell. There was a reason why he'd left her. Something he hadn't told her. Now Sean was going to have to realize that not everything in his life was destined for hell. Nor was every person going to allow him to run away when it suited his purposes—whatever they might be.

Chapter Nine

Morgan stood and came around his large walnut desk as Susannah gave him a slight smile of welcome and stepped into his office. When his assistant, Marie, had shut the door, he opened his arms.

"I'm glad you came, Susannah."

Fighting back tears, Susannah moved into Morgan's comforting embrace. She gave him a quick squeeze of welcome and then stepped away from his towering presence.

"Thanks for seeing me, Morgan. I know how busy you are."

He gestured toward the creamy leather sofa in the corner of the spacious room. "You know you aren't getting out of here without staying at least overnight. Laura insists."

Nervously Susannah sat down. "Yes, I told her I'd stay one night. But she must be terribly busy with this second baby. It's wonderful you have a boy and a girl now."

Morgan nodded, satisfaction in his voice. "A year apart. Katherine Alyssa Trayhern will have a big brother to grow up with. We're very happy about it. She's a real spitfire, too."

Susannah was truly happy for them. Dressed in a navy pin-striped suit, with a paisley silk tie and white shirt, Morgan looked professional, every inch the head of his flourishing company. Susannah and Laura had been close throughout the years, and she knew of Morgan's terrible, torturous past. "Well," she whispered, glancing up at him, "I'm going to need some of that spitfire personality your daughter has."

"I know this involves Killian. How can I help you?" Morgan sat down, alert.

Gripping her leather purse, Susannah held his curious gaze. "I know I was vague on the phone, but I didn't feel this was something I wanted to talk about in detail to anyone except you. And I wanted to do it in person. As I told you on the phone, the school is giving me a month to get my life back in order, and I intend to use it to do just that."

Morgan nodded. "I'm just glad the contract's been lifted. What's this about Killian?"

Susannah's heart contracted in grief. Unable to hold his warm, probing gaze, she felt a lump forming in her throat.

Morgan leaned over and slid his hand across her slumped shoulder. "What's going on, Susannah?"

Fighting to keep herself together, she whispered, "I don't know how it happened or when it happened, but I've fallen in love with Sean." She gave him a pained look. "It happened so fast...."

Morgan nodded. "I fell in love with Laura the first moment I saw her, although I didn't know it then." He grimaced. "I fought the attraction, the love she brought out in me, for a long time. It was nearly my undoing. Luckily, she hung in there and refused to let me go my own way."

"Mercenaries must all be alike," Susannah muttered unhappily.

"There's probably a grain of truth to that. I met Killian in the Foreign Legion. Did you know that?"

"No, I didn't."

"He was a corporal in the company I helped run." Morgan shrugged. "Many of the men I employ here at Perseus are old contacts out of the Legion. The women who work for me all have a military background of some sort, too."

"What is Sean running from?"

"I don't know. Did he tell you anything about his past? He's always been more tight-lipped about it than most."

"No, it's like pulling teeth to get any kind of information out of him." Susannah sat quietly, staring down at her clasped hands. Softly she said, "Something happened to me when Sean was there protecting me from that hit man. The night we were almost killed, I discovered that I loved him. The fact that we might both lose our lives clarified my feelings for him."

Frowning, Morgan sat up. "I see...."

"Sean ran away from me, Morgan. He left me a note. He couldn't even face me to say goodbye, and that's not fair to me—or to him."

"Men who join the Foreign Legion are always running from something," Morgan said gently.

"I understand that now, but that's not an excuse for his behavior. I need some information," Susannah said firmly. "About Sean. About his past."

Morgan opened his hands. "When men come from the Legion, you don't ask many questions," he said gently. "Each of my employees signs a legal document saying that they aren't wanted criminals in another country before I'll hire them for Perseus. It's their word. I don't make inquiries unless I get a tip-off from Interpol or some other governmental body." He shrugged. "And Killian has been one of the most closemouthed of my men. I know very little of his past."

"Then let me fill you in," Susannah whispered, "because when I'm done with my story I want you to tell me where he lives. He and I have some unfinished business to clear up."

Morgan was scowling heavily by the time Susannah had completed her story. He'd asked Marie to bring in hot tea and cookies, and the tray sat on the glass-topped coffee table in front of the sofa. He'd also had her stop all incoming calls—except for emergencies—and canceled the rest of the day's business.

Susannah couldn't eat, but she did sip some fragrant tea.

"I hate to tell you this," Morgan said, sitting down with her again, "but when Killian came in off your assignment he requested leave."

"Leave?"

"Yes. It's a program I devised when I set up this company. When an operative's out in the field, there are tremendous stresses on him or her. When they come in off a particularly demanding assignment, they can request time off from the company for as long as they need to recuperate. Killian came back from Kentucky and wanted leave. I granted it to him, no questions asked."

Susannah's heart beat a little harder. "Where is he, then?"

"Ordinarily, where our people live is top secret. We never give out addresses to anyone, for fear of the information leaking into enemy hands. But in this case, I'm going to make an exception."

Relief made her shaky. "He won't be expecting me to show up."

Morgan smiled grimly. "There's something about the element of surprise—you might catch him off guard enough to level with you."

"He never has leveled with me, Morgan."

Moving uncomfortably, he said, "Susannah, you're dealing with a lot of unknown factors here."

"He's hurting terribly, Morgan."

Rubbing his jaw, Morgan nodded. "I was hurting a lot when Laura met me," he murmured. "And I can't say I was the world's nicest person around her."

"But you hung in there—together. And look at you now. You're happy, Morgan."

Exhaling, he said, "Susannah, Killian's hurting in a lot of ways neither of us knows. I know you're an idealist, and I know you have a large, forgiving heart. But Killian may not have the capacity to reach out to you, even if he wants to. He may be too afraid, for whatever reason. You have to be prepared to accept that if it happens."

She hung her head and nodded. "I'm not so idealistic that I don't know when I'm not wanted, Morgan. But Sean never gave me that chance. He never had the courage to sit down and tell me the truth."

"I'm not saying what he did was right," Morgan said, frowning heavily. "We all run in our own way. Luckily, I had Laura's steadfast courage, her belief in me that helped me get a handhold on my own internal problems." Then, with a slight smile filled with sorrow, he added, "I still have problems that overflow into our personal life, our relationship. Mostly because of me, because of my past that still haunts me. It's not as bad now, but believe me, Laura has her hands full some days with me when the past hits me like a sledgehammer." He glanced at the gold watch on his wrist. "Come on, it's time to go home. Laura promised me a special meal because you were coming. Let's not be late."

The loneliness Susannah had felt since Killian's abrupt departure was somewhat ameliorated by Morgan and his happy family. Laura, beautiful as ever with her long blond hair, dancing eyes and ready smile, helped lift Susannah's spirits. Her son, Jason Charles Trayhern, had his father's dark black hair and gray eyes. On the other hand, three-month-old Katherine Alyssa was a duplicate of Laura's ethereal beauty. Just getting to hold her was a treat for Susannah.

After the meal was eaten and the children had been put to bed, Susannah lingered over a cup of coffee with Laura in the living room. Morgan discreetly excused himself and retired to his home office in the basement of their large home.

Laura curled up on the flowery print couch and smoothed her long pink cotton skirt.

"So tell me what's going on, Susannah! You barely ate any of that great supper I fixed!"

"I know, and I'm really sorry, Laura. The roast leg of lamb was wonderful. It's just that I've got a lot of things on my mind. Well . . . my heart, to be more honest." She smiled and leaned over, petting Sasha, the family's huge brown-and-white Saint Bernard, who had made herself at home next to Susannah's feet. She'd long since taken off her shoes and gotten comfortable—Laura and Morgan's home invited that kind of response.

"Killian, by any chance?"

"How did you know?"

With a slight smile, Laura said softly, "He's a man who's crying for a woman to help bring him out of his self-imposed exile."

"You've always had such insight into people."

Laura shrugged and smiled. "That's what helped me understand Morgan when I first met him. He was a man trapped in hell, although I didn't understand why for quite some time."

"Well," Susannah muttered. "That's exactly how Sean described himself."

"Chances are," Laura said gently, "he lives in an emotional hell on a daily basis." With a sigh, she sipped the coffee. "Susannah, men who go through a war like Morgan did are scarred for life. It kills a part of them, so they're crippled emotionally, in a sense. But that doesn't mean they can't make the most of what is still intact within them."

"Morgan had you to help him realize all of that."

"We had our love, our belief in each other," Laura agreed quietly. "Sometimes it's still not easy. For Morgan, the war will never really be over. There are days when there's a lot of tension between us." She smiled softly. "Fortunately, we love each other enough to sit down and discuss what's bothering him. Morgan has slowly been opening up more with each year that passes, but it's never easy for us, Susannah."

"You have his trust," Susannah pointed out. "I never had time to get Sean's trust. It all happened so fast, so soon...."

"I understand better than most," Laura whispered. "Men like Killian and Morgan need a woman with strength, with steadiness, because they've lost those things emotionally within themselves. I hope you're prepared for the kind of uphill battles a man like that will put you through."

Susannah glanced at her. "You're not scaring me off, Laura, if that's what you're trying to do."

Reaching over, Laura touched her shoulder. "No one believes in the power of love more than I do. I've seen it work miracles with Morgan—and with me." She lifted her head and looked toward the darkened hall that led to the bedrooms, her eyes misty. "And we have two beautiful babies that reflect that love."

"Ma didn't raise me to think life was easy," Susannah said. "I know the hell I went through with Sean while he was there. He just wouldn't—couldn't—talk."

"And that's going to be the biggest stumbling block when you see him again. Men like that feel as if they're carrying such a horrendous amount of ugliness within them. They're afraid that if they start to talk about it, it will get out of control."

"So they get tight-lipped about it?"

Laura nodded. "Exactly."

With a sigh, Susannah shrugged. "I don't have a choice in this, Laura. I don't want one, anyway. Sean is worth it."

"Well, tomorrow morning, Morgan's driver will take you to the airport, and you'll fly to Victoria, British Columbia, where he lives. It's on a lovely island off the west coast of Canada. There's quite a British flavor to the place. And flowers!" Laura smiled fondly. "The island is a riot of color and fragrance. I've never seen so many roses! You'll love the island."

As she listened, Susannah hoped that her lack of worldliness wouldn't be her undoing. She sat tensely, her hands clasped in her lap. All she had to lead her through this tangled web that Sean lived within was her heart. What would he do when she showed up at his doorstep? As Morgan had said, the element of surprise might work for her—but, she thought, it could also work against her.

Susannah had never needed the kind of strength she knew she would need in order to face Sean Killian bravely. Only Sean could show her if what she felt for him was love. But even if it was, there was no guarantee that he would have the courage to admit it.

Kneeling in the triangular flower bed, Killian stared glumly down at the bright yellow marigold in his hands. The gold, red and yellow flowers assaulted the air with their rather acrid odor. Like the flower in his hand, surrounded by the moist, rich soil, he was alone. Alone and bitter.

Resolutely he dug a small hole with the trowel, and placed the marigold in it. With dirt-stained hands, he pressed the moist earth securely over the roots. Gardening had always helped soothe him. *Until now.*

Looking up from the garden, Killian stared at the calm blue of the ocean, three hundred feet away. His green manicured lawn contrasted beautifully with the glassy water. The pale azure of the sky was dotted with fleecy white clouds. Summer in Victoria was his favorite time. Luckily, the money he'd earned over the years had gotten him this small English-style cottage when the couple who'd owned it, up in years, could no longer keep up with its landscaping and gardening demands and sold it to him.

Susannah. Her name hung in front of Killian as he caressed the tiny, frilly petals of a pale yellow marigold. The color reminded him of the hope that always burned in her eyes. Hope. He had none. The feeling had been utterly destroyed so long ago. Closing his eyes, he knelt there, surrounded by the lonely cries of the sea gulls that endlessly patrolled the beach and, off in the distance, the hoarse barks of sea lions.

Killian opened his eyes, feeling the terrible loneliness knife through him as never before. Slowly he looked around. He was surrounded by the ephemeral beauty of many carefully constructed flower beds, all geometrically shaped and designed by him, their rainbow colors breathtaking. But Killian could feel none of his usual response to them. Only Susannah could make him feel.

What was wrong? What had happened to him? He opened up his hands and studied them darkly. He'd made love to other women off and on throughout his life, but never had the act—or more truthfully, the feelings—continued to live like a burning-hot light within his body and heart as they did now.

With a shake of his head, Killian muttered under his breath and got to his feet. Brushing off the bits of soil clinging to his jeans, he straightened. The three tiers of flower gardens culminated with at least a hundred roses of various colors. Their fragrance was heavy in the area nearest the rear sliding glass doors to his house.

And it was a house, Killian reminded himself harshly. Susannah's ramshackle, broken-down old place was a *home*. She'd made it feel homey, comfortable and warm with her life and presence. Killian savored the hours spent with her in that antiquated kitchen. Every night when he lay down to try to sleep, those scenes would replay like a haunting movie across his closed eyelids. And when he finally did sleep, torrid, heated dreams of loving Susannah drove him to wakefulness, and a clawing hunger that brought him to the verge of tears. Tears! He never cried!

Stopping at the rose garden, a long, rectangular area bordered with red brick, Killian barely brushed a lavender rose with his fingertips. *Susannah*. No longer did Killian try to escape her memory. The doorbell rang, pulling his attention from his morbid reverie. Who could it be? His housekeeper and regular gardener, Emily Johnston, had left earlier to buy the week's groceries, and she wouldn't be back until tomorrow morning.

Automatically Killian dropped into his natural mode of wariness. Although his address and phone number were known only to Meg and Morgan, he didn't trust his many enemies not to track him down. As careful as Killian was about masking his movements to preserve his sanctuary, he never fooled himself. Someday one of his more patient and vengeful enemies might locate him.

Padding through the fully carpeted house, Killian halted at the front door and peered through the one-way glass. *Susannah!* His heart thumped hard in his chest. What the hell was she doing here? Could he be dreaming? His mind spun with questions. His heart began an uneven pounding. As he closed his hand over the brass doorknob, Killian felt a surge of hope tunnel through him. Just as quickly, he savagely destroyed the burgeoning feeling.

The door swung open. Susannah looked through the screen at Killian. As usual, his features were set—but his eyes gave away his true feelings. Her palms were sweaty, and her heart was thundering like a runaway freight train. She girded herself for his disapproval.

"What are you doing here?" Killian demanded in a rasp. He glanced around, checking out the surrounding area. Luckily, the street ended in a cul-de-sac, and he knew who his neighbors were and the cars they drove. The white Toyota out front must be a rental car that Susannah had driven.

"We've got some unfinished business," Susannah whispered. It was so hard to gather strength when she felt like caving in and stepping those precious few feet to fall into Killian's arms. The terrible light in his eyes told him he was no less tortured by her unexpected appearance than she was.

"Get in here," he growled, and gripped her by the arm.

Susannah didn't resist. She could tell that Killian was carefully monitoring the amount of strength he applied to her arm. She entered his home. A dusky-rose carpet flowed throughout the living room and hall area, which was decorated with simple, spare, carefully placed furniture. The walls were covered with floor-to-ceiling bookcases. Killian must be a voracious reader.

There were so many impressions she wanted to absorb, to investigate. Each one would give her another clue to Killian. But she didn't have that kind of time. Every word, every gesture, counted. She turned as he closed the door with finality. The grimness in his face made her feel cold. Alone.

"How did you find me?"

"I flew to Washington and talked with Morgan. He told me where you lived." Susannah saw his eyes flare with disbelief.

Killian took a step back, because if he didn't he was going to sweep Susannah uncompromisingly into his arms. And then he was going to take her to his bedroom and make wild, hungry love with her until they were so exhausted that they couldn't move.

Killian looked down at her vulnerable features. There was real hope in Susannah's eyes, a kind of hope he'd never be able to claim as his own. She was dressed in a summery print blouse—pink peonies against a white background—and white slacks, with sandals outlining her feet. Her lovely sable hair was trapped in a chignon, and Killian had to stop himself from reaching forward to release that captive mass of silk into his hands. His mouth had grown dry, and his heart was beating dangerously hard in his chest.

"All right, what's going on?"

"You and me." Susannah felt her fear almost overwhelming her, but she dared not be weak now. She saw a slight thawing in Killian's narrowed eyes, a slight softening of his thinned mouth. "What made you think," Susannah said in a low, strangled voice, "that you could walk out on me just like that? We made love with each other, Sean. I thought—I thought we meant something to each other." She forced herself to hold his hardening gaze. "You ran without ever giving me the opportunity to sit down and talk to you. I'm here to complete unfinished business." Her voice grew hoarse. "One way or another."

Killian stood stunned. It took him a long time to find his voice. "I told you—I didn't mean to hurt you," he rasped. "I thought leaving the way I did would hurt you less."

Susannah's eyes went round, and anger gave her the backbone she needed. "Hurt me less?" Susannah forced herself to walk into the living room. She dropped her purse and her one piece of luggage on the carpet. Turning, she rounded on Killian. "I don't call running out on me less hurtful!"

Nervously Killian shoved his hands into the pockets of his jeans. "I'm sorry, Susannah. For everything."

"For loving me?"

Killian dropped his gaze and stared at the floor. He heard the ache in her husky tone; her voice was like a lover's caress. He was glad to see her, glad that she was here. "No," he admitted. He raised his chin and forced himself to meet her large, tear-filled eyes. "But I am sorry for the hurt I've caused you."

"You walk around in your silence and don't communicate worth a darn. I'm not a mind reader. Do you know how awful I felt after you left? Do you know that I blamed myself? I asked myself what I did wrong. Was it something I said? Did?" Grimly, her eyes flashing, she said, "I don't have a lot of worldly ways like you. I know I'm a country woman, but I don't question the way of my heart, Sean. You had no right to leave the way you did. It wasn't fair to me, and it wasn't fair to you, either."

Pain knifed through him and he moved into the living room with her. He halted a foot away from her, aching to put his hands on her shoulders, but not daring to. "I was to blame, not you."

To her amazement, Susannah saw Killian thawing. Perhaps Laura was right: He needed a woman to be stronger than him so that he could feel safe enough to open up. Had he never had a woman of strength to lean on? If not, it was no wonder he remained closed, protecting his vulnerability. The discovery was as sweet as it was bold—and frightening. Susannah was just coming out of her own trauma. Did she have enough strength for the both of them? She simply didn't know, but the glimmer in Killian's eyes, the way his mouth unconsciously hinted at the vulnerability he tried so hard to hide and protect, made her decide to try anyway.

"I hope you've got a guest bedroom."

He blinked.

Susannah drilled him with a fiery look. "Sean, I happen to feel that we meant a lot to each other when you were in Kentucky. And after we made love, you ran. I don't know your reasons for running, and that's what I'm here to find out. I intend to stay here, no matter how miserable you make it for me, until we get to the bottom of this—together."

Dread flared through Killian. No woman had ever challenged him like this. "You don't know what you're saying," he warned.

"Like heck I don't! Give me some credit, Sean. I work with special children. I've got to have a lot of insight into them to reach them, to touch them, so that they'll stop retreating."

Killian took another step away, terror warring with his need of Susannah. "You're biting off too much. You don't know what you're getting into," he snapped.

Tilting her chin, Susannah rasped, "Oh, yes I do."

"Now look," he said in a low, gravelly voice, "I don't want to hurt you, Susannah. If you stay here, it'll happen. Don't put yourself on the firing line for me. I'm not worth it."

Tears stung her eyes, but Susannah forced them back. Killian would read her tears as a sign of weakness. "You're wrong. You're a good man, Sean. You've been hurt, and you're hiding. I'm here to show you that you don't need to keep running. You're allowed to laugh, you know. And to cry. How long has it been since you've done either?''

Killian lunged forward blindly and gripped her by the arm. ''Dammit,'' he rasped off-key, ''get the hell out of here while you still can, Susannah! I'm a monster! A monster!'' He savagely poked a finger at his belly. ''It's in here, this thing, this hell that I carry. It comes out and controls me, and it will hurt whoever is around. You've got to understand that!''

She held his blazing gaze, seeing the horror of his past reflected in his eyes, hearing the anguish in his tone. ''No,'' she said. ''I'm not afraid of you,'' she rattled, ''or that so-called monster inside of you. For the first time in your life, Sean, you're going to be honest, not only with yourself, but with someone else—me.''

Killian took a step back, as if she'd slapped him. He stared down at her as the tension swirled around them like a raging storm. Frightened as never before, he backed away. In place of the panic came anger. He ground out, ''If you stay, you stay at your own risk. Do you understand that?''

''I do.''

He glared at her. ''You're naive and idealistic. I'll hurt you in ways you never thought possible! I won't mean to, but it'll happen, Susannah.'' He stood there, suddenly feeling very old and broken. His voice grew hoarse. ''I don't want to, but I will. God help me, I don't want to hurt you, Susannah.''

Swallowing hard, a lump forming in her throat, she nodded. ''I know,'' she replied softly, ''I know....''

"This is hopeless," Killian whispered, looking out one of the series of plate-glass windows that faced the flower gardens and the ocean. "I'm hopeless."

Grimly Susannah fought the desire to take Killian into her arms. Intuitively she understood that it would weaken her position with him. He was wary and defensive enough to strike out verbally and hurt her for fear of getting hurt again. As she picked up her luggage, Susannah realized that her love for Sean was the gateway not only to trust, but also to a wealth of yet-untapped affection that lay deep within her.

"You're not hopeless," Susannah told him gently. "Now, if you'll show me where the guest bedroom is, I'll get settled in."

Killian gaped at her. His mouth opened, then closed. "First door on the right down the hall," he muttered, then spun on his heel and left.

Her hands shaking, Susannah put her week's worth of clothes away in the closet and the dresser. Her heart wouldn't steady, but a clean feeling, something akin to a sense of victory, soared within her. She took several deep breaths to calm herself after having established a beachhead in the initial confrontation. Killian's desperation told her, she hoped, how much he was, indeed, still tied to her. Perhaps Morgan and Laura were right, and Killian did love her after all. That was the only thing that could possibly pull them through this storm together. Any less powerful emotion would surely destroy her, and continue to wound Killian.

Straightening up from her task, Susannah took in the simple, spare room. A delicate white Irish lace spread covered the double bed. The carpet was pale lavender, and the walls cream-colored. A vibrant Van Gogh print of sunflowers hung above the bed. The maple dresser was surely an antique, but Susannah didn't know from what era. The window, framed by lavender drapes and ivory sheers, overlooked a breathtaking view of the ocean.

"Well, Susannah, keep going," she warned herself. As much as she wanted to hide in the bedroom, she knew it wasn't the answer. No, she had to establish herself as a force in Killian's isolated world, and make herself part of it—whether he wanted her to or not. And in her heart she sensed that he did want her. The risk to her heart was great. But her love for Killian was strong enough to let her take that risk. He was always risking his life for others; well, it was time someone took a risk for him.

Killian stole a look into the kitchen. Susannah had busied herself all afternoon in his spacious modern kitchen. Although he'd hidden out most of the time in the garage, working on a wood-carving project, the fragrant odors coming from the kitchen couldn't be ignored. As upset as he was, the food she was cooking made him hungry. But it was his other hunger for Susannah that he was trying to quell—and he wasn't succeeding.

"What's for dinner?" he asked with a frown.

Susannah wiped her hands on the dark green apron she had tied around her waist. "Pot roast with sour-cream gravy and biscuits. Southerners love their biscuits and gravy," she said with pride.

"Sounds decent. Dessert?" He glanced at her.

"You really push your luck, don't you?"

He wanted to smile, but couldn't. "Yeah, I guess I do."

"I didn't come here to be a slave who cooks you three meals a day and cleans your house," Susannah pointed out as she gestured for him to sit down at the table. "This food is going to cost you."

"Oh?" Thinking he should leave, Killian sat down. Susannah seemed to belong in the kitchen—her presence was like sunshine. The bleakness of his life seemed to dissolve in her aura.

Susannah served the meat and placed the pitcher of gravy on the table with a basket of homemade biscuits. Sitting down, she held his inquiring gaze. "My folks and I always used to sit and talk after meals. It was one of the most important things I learned from them—talking."

With a grimace, Killian offered her the platter of meat first. "I'm not much of one for talking and you know it."

"So you'll learn to become a better communicator," Susannah said lightly. She felt absolutely tied in knots, and she had to force herself to put food on her plate. Just being this close to Killian, to his powerful physical presence, was making her body betray her head. When his lips curved into that sour smile, Susannah melted inwardly. She remembered how hot, how demanding and sharing, that mouth had been on hers. Never had she wanted to kiss a man so much. But she knew if she bowed to her selfish hunger for him as a man, she'd lose not only the battle, but the war, as well.

"Okay," he said tentatively, "you want me to talk." He spooned several thick portions of the roast onto his plate, added three biscuits and then some gravy. "About what?"

"You," Susannah said pointedly.

"I'm willing to talk about anything else," he warned her heavily.

With a shrug, Susannah said, "Fine. Start anywhere you want."

The food was delectable, and Killian found himself wolfing down the thick, juicy meat. Still in wonder over this strong, stubborn side of Susannah that he hadn't seen before, he shook his head.

"I didn't realize you were this persistent."

Susannah grinned. "Would it have changed anything?"

The merest shadow of a smile touched Killian's mouth, and the hesitant, pain-filled attempt sent a sheet of heat through Susannah. Taking a deep breath, she said, "I want to know about you, your past, Sean. I don't think that's too much to ask. It will help me understand you—and, maybe, myself, and how I feel toward you."

Again her simple honesty cut through him. He ate slowly, not only hearing, but also feeling her words. He saw Susannah's hands tremble ever so slightly. She was nervous, perhaps even more nervous than he was. Still, his heart filled with such joy that she was here that it took the edge off his terror. "So, if I open up, maybe you'll give me some of that dessert you made?"

Susannah laughed, feeling her first glimmer of hope. She felt Killian testing her, seeing if she was really as strong as he needed her to be. "That coconut chiffon pie is going to go to waste if you don't start talking, Sean Killian."

Her laughter was like sunlight in his dark world. In that moment, her eyes sparkling, her lush mouth curved, Killian ached to love her, ached to feel her take away his darkness. Hope flickered deep within him, and it left him nonplussed. Never had he experienced this feeling before. Not like this. Giving her an annoyed look, he muttered, "I'd rather talk about my flower gardens, and the roses."

"Enough about the roses," Susannah said as she stood up and cleared away the dishes. She saw his eyes darken instantly. Tightening her lips, she went to the refrigerator, pulled out the pie and cut two slices.

"I want you to tell me about your childhood."

Moodily he sat back in the chair, unable to tear his gaze from her. "It's not a very happy story" was all he said.

Susannah gave him a piece of pie and a fork. She sat back down, grimly holding his hooded gaze. "Tell me about it."

With a sigh, Killian shrugged and picked up the fork. "I was the runt. The kid who was too small for his age. I was always scrapping with older boys who thought they could push my younger sister Meg around. He pointed to his crooked nose. "I had this busted on three different occasions in grade school."

"Did you have anyone to hold you?"

Killian flashed her an amused look. "Scrappers didn't fall into their mothers' arms and cry, Susannah."

"Is your mother alive?"

He winced inwardly and scowled, paying a lot of attention to his pie, which he hadn't touched. "Mother died when I was fourteen."

"What did she die of?" Susannah asked softly.

Rearing back in the chair, and wiping his hands absently on his jeans, Killian replied, "A robbery."

She heard the rising pain in Killian's tone, and saw it in the slash of his mouth. "Tell me about it."

"Not much to tell," he muttered. "When I was thirteen, my parents emigrated to America. They set up a grocery store in the Bronx. A year later, a couple of kids came in to rob them. They took the money and killed my parents," he concluded bluntly. Killian bowed his head, feeling the hot rush of tears in his tightly shut eyes. Then he felt Susannah's hand fall gently on his shoulder. Just that simple gesture of solace nearly broke open the wall of grief he'd carried so long over his parents' harsh and unjust deaths.

Fighting to keep her own feelings under control, Susannah tried to understand what that experience would do to a fourteen-year-old boy, an immigrant. "You were suddenly left alone," she said unsteadily. "And Meg was younger?"

"Yes, by a year."

Susannah could feel the anguish radiating from him. "What did you do?"

Killian fought the urge to put his hand over hers where it lay on his shoulder. If he did, he'd want to bury his head blindly against her body and sob. The lump in his throat grew. So many unbidden, unexpected feelings sheared through him. Desperate, not understanding how Susannah could so easily pull these emotions out of him and send them boiling to the surface, Killian choked. With a growl, he lunged away from the table, and his chair fell to the tiled floor.

"You have no right to do this to me. None!" He turned and jerked the chair upright.

Susannah sat very still, working to keep her face neutral. She battled tears, and prayed that Killian couldn't see them in her eyes. His face was pale and tense, and his eyes were haunted.

"If you're smart," he rasped as he headed toward the garden, "you'll leave right now, Susannah."

Stubbornly she shook her head. "I'm staying, Sean."

His fingers gripped the doorknob. "Damn you! Damn you—"

She closed her eyes and took a deep, ragged breath. "You aren't going to scare me off."

"Then you'd better lock the door to your bedroom tonight," he growled. "I want you so damned bad I can taste it. I can taste you." He jabbed his finger warningly at her. "You keep this up, and I don't know what will happen. You're not safe here with me. Don't you understand?"

Susannah turned in her chair. When she spoke, her voice was soft. "You're not even safe with yourself, Sean."

Wincing, he stalked out of the house. Maybe a walk, a long, brutal walk, would cleanse his agitated soul and his bleeding heart. He loved Susannah, yet he feared he'd hurt her. No woman had ever unstrung him as easily and quickly as she did. He strode through the beauty of his flower gardens, unseeing.

Chapter Ten

Susannah got ready for bed. She hadn't heard Killian return, and it was nearly eleven. Her nerves were raw, and she was jangled.

Lock the door.

Did she want to? Could she say no if Killian came into her bedroom? Where did running and hiding end? And where did freedom, for both of them, begin? Perhaps it would be born out of the heat of their mutual love.... Her hands trembling, Susannah pulled down the bed covers. The room was dark now. Slivers of moonlight pierced the curtains, lending a muted radiance to the room.

Lock the door.

Dressed in a simple knee-length cotton gown, Susannah pulled the brush through her hair. Her own emotions were jumbled and skittish. What if Sean walked through that door? She stared hard at the doorknob. She hadn't locked it—yet. Should she? Was she hesitating for herself or for Sean?

Lock the door.

Trying to recall the nights with Killian at her farmhouse, Susannah realized that she'd been in such turmoil herself that, except for that one night, she had no idea if he generally slept, had terrible nightmares or experienced insomnia. Making a small sound of frustration, she set the tortoiseshell brush on the dresser. No. No, she had to leave the door open. If she locked it, it was a symbol that she really didn't trust him—or herself. Taking a deep, unsteady breath, she slipped between the cool sheets. Getting comfortable, she lay there, her hands behind her head, for a long, long time—waiting. Just waiting.

Lock the door.

Killian moved like a ghost through his own house. All the lights were out, but the moon provided just enough light to see. He was sweaty and tired, having walked miles along the beach in order to purge himself of the awful roiling emotions that were flaying him alive. The forced hike had taken the edge off him, but he hadn't dealt at all with his feelings.

Susannah.

Killian stood frozen in the hallway and finally faced the full realization: He loved her. His hand shook as he touched his forehead. When? Making a sound of disgust, he thought that from the moment he'd seen Susannah his heart had become a traitor to him. Yes, he'd made love to women in his life, but never had he wanted truly to love them. With Susannah, he wanted to give. He wanted to see that velvet languor in her eyes, and the soft curve of her lips as he pleasured her, loved her so thoroughly that they fused into melting oneness.

His nerves raw, more exhausted than he could recall ever having been, Killian forced himself to go to his room for a cold shower. But as he passed Susannah's room, he stopped. His eyes narrowed on the doorknob. Had she done as he ordered and locked her door against him? Sweat stood out on his tense features as his hand slowly moved forward. For an instant, his fingers hovered. A part of him wanted her to have the door locked. He didn't want to hurt her—didn't want to take from her without giving something back. But how could he give, when he didn't even know how to give to himself after all those years?

His mouth tightening, Killian's hand flowed around the doorknob. He twisted it gently. It was unlocked! He stood there, filled with terror and hope, filled with such hunger and longing that he couldn't move. Susannah trusted him. She trusted him to do the right thing for both of them. Just as quietly, he eased the doorknob back to its original position.

Her heart beating wildly, Susannah sensed Killian's presence outside her room. She lay there gripping the sheet, her eyes wide, as she watched the doorknob slowly turn, trying to prepare herself emotionally. If he entered her room, she wasn't sure what she'd do. Her heart whispered to her to love him, to hold him, to allow him to spend himself within her. Loving was healing, and Susannah knew that instinctively. Her head warned her sharply that he'd use her up and eventually destroy her emotionally, just as he'd been destroyed himself over the years.

The seconds ticked by, and Susannah watched the doorknob twist back into place. Killian knew now that she was accessible, that she would be here for him, for whatever he needed from her. The thought was as frightening as it was exhilarating. On one level, Susannah felt as if she were dealing with a wild, unmanageable animal that would just as soon hurt her as stay with her. That was the wounded side of Sean. The other side, the man who possessed such poignant sensitivity and awareness of her as a woman, was very different. Somewhere in the careening thoughts that clashed with her overwrought feelings, Susannah was counting on that other part of Sean to surface. But would it? And in time?

When the door didn't open, she drew in a shaky breath of air and gradually relaxed. At least Killian had come home. She'd worried about where he'd gone, and indeed whether he'd return. Forcing her eyes closed, Susannah felt some of the tension drain from her arms and legs. Sleep. She had to get some sleep. Tomorrow morning would be another uphill battle with Sean. But the night was young, her mind warned her. What were Killian's sleeping habits? Was he like a beast on the prowl, haunted by ghosts of the past, unable to sleep at night? Susannah wished she knew.

Sometime later, her eyelids grew heavy, her heart settled down, and she snuggled into the pillow. Almost immediately, she began to dream of Sean, and their conversation at the table—and the look of pain he carried in his eyes.

* * *

Susannah jerked awake. Her lips parting, she twisted her head from one side to the other. Had she been dreaming? Had she heard a scream? Or perhaps more the sound of an animal crying out than a human scream? Fumbling sleepily, she threw off the sheet and the bedspread. Dream or reality? She had to find out. What time was it? Stumbling to her feet, Susannah bumped into the dresser.

"Ouch!" she muttered, wiping the sleep from her eyes. Her hair, in disarray, settled around her face as she glanced at the clock. It was 3:00 a.m. The moonlight had shifted considerably, and the room was darker now than before. Reaching for her robe, Susannah struggled into it.

She stepped out into the hall, but only silence met her sensitive hearing. Killian's room was across the hall. The door was partly open. Her heart starting a slow, hard pounding, Susannah forced herself to move toward it.

Just as she reached it, she heard a muffled crash in another part of the house. Startled, she turned and moved on bare feet down the carpeted hall toward the sound. In the center of the gloom-ridden living room, she halted. Her nerves taut, her breathing suspended, Susannah realized that the sounds were coming from the garage. Killian did woodworking out there. More crashes occurred. Fear snaked through her. She knew he was out there. She had to go to him. She had to confront him. Now Susannah understood what an animal trainer must feel like, facing a wild, untamed animal.

Her mouth dry, her throat constricted and aching, Susannah reached for the doorknob. A flood of light from the garage momentarily blinded her, and she stopped in the doorway, her hand raised to shade her eyes.

Killian whirled around, his breathing raspy and harsh. His eyes narrowed to slits as he picked up the sound of the door leading to the house being opened. He'd prayed that his shrieks wouldn't wake Susannah, but there she stood, looking sleepy yet frightened. Sweat ran down the sides of his face.

"I told you—get the hell out of here!" The words, more plea than threat, tore out of him. "Go! Run!"

Susannah's mouth fell open. Killian's cry careened off the walls of the large woodworking shop. Despite her fear, she noted beautifully carved statues—mostly of children, mothers with children, and flying birds. Some had been knocked off their pedestals and lay strewn across the concrete floor. Were those the crashes she'd heard? Susannah's gaze riveted on Killian. He was naked save for a pair of drawstring pajama bottoms clinging damply to his lower body. His entire torso gleamed in the low light, and his hair was damp and plastered against his skull. More than anything, Susannah saw the malevolent terror in his dark, anguished eyes.

She whispered his name and moved forward.

"No!" Killian pleaded, backing away. "Don't come near me! Damn it, don't!"

Blindly Susannah shook her head, opening her arms to him. "No," she cried softly. "You won't hurt me.

You won't..." and she moved with a purpose that gave her strength and kept her fear in check.

Stumbling backward, Killian was trapped by the wood cabinets. There was no place to turn, no place to run. He saw blips of Susannah interspersed among the violent scenes that haunted him continuously. In one, he saw the enemy coming at him, knife upraised. Another flashback showed his torturer coming forward with a wire to garrote him. He shook his head, a whimper escaping his tightened lips. He was trying desperately to cling to reality, to the fact that Susannah was here with him. He heard her soft, husky voice. He heard the snarl and curse of his enemies as they leaped toward him.

"No!" He threw his hands out in front of him to stop her. Simultaneously the flashback overwhelmed him. His hands were lethal weapons, honed by years of karate training, thickened by calluses, and he moved into position to protect himself. Breathing hard, he waited for his enemy to come at him with the knife as he met and held his dark, angry eyes.

Susannah saw the wildness in Killian's eyes, and she reached out to touch his raised hand. His face was frozen into a mask devoid of emotion; his eyes were fathomless, intent and slitted. Fear rose in her, but she knew she had to confront it, make it her friend and reach Killian, reach inside him.

Just as she grazed his hand, he whimpered. Her eyes widened as she saw him shift.

"Sean, no!" She threw out one hand to try to stop him. "No," she choked out again.

Where was he? He heard Susannah's cry. *Where?* Slowly the flashbacks faded, and Killian realized she was gripping his arm, her eyes wide and brimming with tears.

"No..." he rasped, and quickly jerked away from Susannah's touch. "God...I'm sorry." Bitterness coated his mouth, and he dragged in a ragged breath. "I could have hurt you. My God, I nearly—"

"It's all right. I'm all right, and so are you," Susannah whispered. Dizziness assailed her. She stood very still. When he reached out to touch her, his hand was trembling. The instant Killian's fingers touched her unbound hair, Susannah wanted to cry. There was such anguish in his eyes as he caressed her hair, as if to make sure she wasn't a part of whatever nightmare had held him in its thrall. Gathering what courage she had left, Susannah lifted her hand and caught his. His skin was sweaty, and the thrum of tension was palpable in his grip.

"It was just a nightmare," she quavered, lifting her head and meeting his tortured eyes.

Killian muttered something under his breath. "You shouldn't have stayed," he rasped. "I might have hurt you...." He gently framed her face and looked deeply into her tear-filled eyes. "I'm so afraid, Susannah."

Whispering his name, Susannah slid her arms around him and brought him against her. She heard a harsh sound escape his mouth as he buried his face against her hair, his arms moving like steel bands around her. The air rushed from her lungs, but she relaxed against him, understanding his need to hold and be held.

"I love you," she whispered, sliding her fingers through his short black hair. "I love you...."

Her words, soft and quavering, flowed through Killian. Without thinking, he lifted his head to seek her mouth. Blindly he sought and found her waiting lips. They tasted sweet, soft and giving as he hungrily took her offering. His breathing was chaotic, and so was hers. Drowning in Susannah's mouth and feeling her hands moving reassuringly across his shoulders took away the terror that had inhabited him. Her moan was of pleasure, not pain.

In those stark, naked moments, Killian stopped taking from her and began to give back. Her mouth blossomed beneath his, warm, sweet and hot. How badly he wanted to love her; his body was aching testimony to his need. Tearing his mouth from hers, he held her languorous gray gaze, which now sparkled with joy.

"It's going to be all right," he promised unsteadily. "Everything's going to be all right. Come on...."

Susannah remained beneath his arm, his protection, as he led her through the silent house. In the living room, he guided her to the couch and sat down with her. Their knees touched, and he held both her hands. "You're the last person in the world I'd ever want to hurt," he rasped.

"I know...."

"Dammit, Susannah, why didn't you run? Why didn't you leave me?"

She slowly looked up, meeting and holding his tear-filled eyes. "B-because I love you, Sean. You don't leave someone you love, who's hurting, to suffer the way you were suffering."

Killian closed his eyes and pulled her against him. The moments of silence blended together, and he felt the hotness of tears brim over and begin to course down his cheeks. His hands tightened around her as he gathered her into his arms. Burying his face in her sable hair, he felt a wrenching sob working its way up and out of his gut. The instant her arms went hesitantly around his shoulders, the sob tore from him. His entire body shook in response.

"Go ahead," Susannah whispered, tears in her eyes. "Cry, Sean. Cry for all the awful things you've seen and had to do to survive. Cry. I'll hold you. I'll just hold you...." And she did, with all the womanly strength she possessed.

Time drew to a halt, and all Susannah could feel were the terrible shudders racking Killian's lean body as he clung to her, nearly squeezing the breath from her. He clung as if he feared that to let go would be to be lost forever. Susannah understood that better than most. She tightened her grip around his damp shoulders, whispering words of encouragement, of love, of care, as his sobs grew louder and harsher, wrenching from him.

Susannah was no longer feeling her own pain, she was experiencing his. She held Killian as if she feared that to release him would mean he would break into a million shattered pieces. His fingers dug convulsively into her back as the sobs continued to rip through him. Her gown grew damp, but she didn't care. His ability to trust her, to give himself over to her and release the glut of anguish he'd carried by himself for so long, was exhilarating.

Gradually Killian's sobs lessened, and so did the convulsions that had torn at him in her arms. Gently Susannah stroked his hair, shoulders and back. His spine was strong, and the muscles on either side of it were lean.

"You're going to be fine," Susannah whispered, pressing a kiss against his temple. "Just fine." She sighed, resting her head against his, suddenly exhausted.

Killian flexed his fingers against Susannah's back. Never had he felt more safe—or loved—than now. Just the soft press of her lips against his temple moved him to tears again. He nuzzled deeply into her hair, pressing small kisses against her neck and jaw.

Words wouldn't come. Each stroke of Susannah's hand took a little more of the pain away. The fragrance of her body, the sweetness of it, enveloped him, and he clung to her small, strong form, absorbing the strength she was feeding him through her touch and voice.

Susannah had been hurt by his abruptly leaving her life without an explanation, yet now she was strong, when he had never felt weaker. Her fingers trembled against his hair, and he slowly lifted his head. She gave him a tremulous half smile, her eyes huge with compassion and love for him.

Love. He saw it in every nuance of her expression, in her hand as it came to rest against his jaw. How could she love him? When she reached forward, her fingers taking away the last of the tears from his cheeks, he lowered his lashes, ashamed.

"Tears are wonderful," Susannah whispered, a catch in her voice. "Ma always said they were liquid crystals going back to Mother Earth. I always liked that thought. She said they were the path to the heart, and I know it's true." She smiled gently into Killian's ravaged eyes. "You were brave enough to take the biggest step of all, Sean."

"What do you mean?" he asked, his voice thick, off-key.

"You had the ability to reach out and trust someone with your feelings."

"Crying is a weakness."

"Who taught you that?"

"Father. Men don't cry."

"And they aren't supposed to feel. Oh, Sean—" Susannah stroked his cheek gently. "Men have hearts, too, you know. Hearts that have a right to feel as deeply and widely as any woman's."

He shakily reached over and touched her cheek. "I was afraid that if my nightmares came back and you were around, I'd hurt you." Hanging his head, unable to meet her compassionate gaze, he said, "When I was in the Foreign Legion, I met an Algerian woman, Salima, who loved me. I loved her, too." He shook his head sadly. "I kept having nightmares out of my violent past with the Legion, and it scared her. Finally, I left her for good. I feared that one night I might lash out and strike her." Miserable, Killian held Susannah's gaze. "After that, I swore never to get involved with a woman. I didn't want to put anyone through the hell I put Salima through. I saw what it did to her, and I swore I'd never do it again. And then you walked into my life. I've never felt such strong emotions for a woman before, Susannah. Those old fears made me leave to protect you from what I might do some night. My God, I couldn't stand it if I hurt you. I nearly did tonight."

She caressed his jaw. "You could have, but you didn't. Some part of you knew it was me, Sean. That's what stopped you, darling."

He lowered his gaze, his voice cracking. "I—I had a nightmare about Peru, about one of our missions. Wolf and I got caught and tortured by a drug lord, and the rest of our team had to go into the estate and bust us out." He squeezed his eyes shut. "That was last year. It's too fresh—that's why I get these nightmares, the flashbacks . . ."

"And you were having flashbacks after you woke up?" Susannah guessed grimly.

His mouth quirked and he raised his head. "Yes. I was hoping . . ." He drew in a ragged sigh. "I started screaming in my bedroom, and I got up, hoping I hadn't awakened you. I went out to the garage, where I always go when these things hit. It's safer that way. A lot safer. I'm like a wild animal in a cage," Killian added bitterly, unable to meet her lustrous gaze. His hands tightened around hers.

"A wounded animal, but not a wild one," she whispered achingly as she cupped his cheek. Killian's eyes were bleak; there was such sadness reflected in them, and in the line of his mouth. "Wounds can be bound up to heal, Sean."

He managed a soft snort. "At what cost to the healer?"

Susannah stroked his damp, bristly cheek. The dark growth of beard gave his face a dangerous quality. "As long as you're willing to get help, to make the necessary changes, then I can stay with you, if you want."

He turned to her. "Look at you. Look at the price you've already paid."

Susannah nodded. "It was worth the price, Sean. *You're* worth the effort. Don't you understand that?"

"I don't know what kind of miracle was at work when you reached out for me," he rasped. Killian held up his hands. "I've killed with these, Susannah. And when I mean to defend myself, I do it. The other person doesn't survive."

A chill swept through Susannah as she stared at his lean, callused hands. Swallowing convulsively, she whispered, "Some part of you knew I wasn't your enemy, Sean."

He wanted to say, *I love you, that's why,* but stopped himself. Just looking at her pale, washed-out features told him that he had no right to put Susannah on the firing line. A terrible need to make love with her, to speak of his love for her courage, her strength, sheared through Killian. He gazed down at her innocent, upturned face.

"You're a beautiful idealist," he whispered unsteadily. "Someone I don't deserve, and never will."

"I'll decide those things for myself."

He gave her a strange look, but said nothing. Placing his hand on her shoulder, he rasped, "Let's get you to bed. You need some sleep."

"And you? What about you?"

He shrugged. "I won't sleep."

"You slept like a baby after we made love to each other," Susannah whispered. She reached over and gripped his hand.

"I guess I did."

Susannah held his misery-laden eyes. "Then sleep with me now."

Killian stared at her, the silence lengthening between them. His throat constricted.

"Come," she whispered. "Come sleep at my side."

Chapter Eleven

A ragged sigh tore from Killian as he felt Susannah's weight settle against him. The darkness in her bedroom was nearly complete. Everything was so natural between them that it hurt. Despite how badly he'd frightened Susannah, she laid her head in the hollow of his shoulder, and her body met and melded against the harder contours of his. Her arm went around his torso, and Killian heard a quivering sigh issue from her lips. To his alarm, after he'd drawn up the sheet and spread, he felt Susannah trembling. It wasn't obvious, but Killian sensed it was adrenaline letdown after the trauma she'd endured.

"This is heaven on earth," he whispered roughly against her hair, tightening his grip around her. Susannah was heaven. A heaven he didn't deserve.

"It is." Susannah sighed and unconsciously moved her hand across his naked chest. The hair there was soft and silky. His groan reverberated through her like music. Stretching upward, Susannah placed her lips softly against the hardened line of his mouth. Instantly Killian tensed, and his mouth opened and hungrily devoured hers. She surrendered herself to the elemental fire that leaped between them wherever their bodies touched.

Sean needed to understand that no matter how bad the terror that lived within him was, her love—and what she hoped was his love for her—could meet and dissolve it. Susannah's fleeting thought was quickly drowned in the splendor of his mouth as it captured hers with a primal hunger that sent heat twisting and winding through her. His hands tangled in her thick hair, and he gently eased her back on the pillow, his blue eyes narrowed and glittering.

"Love sets you free," she said, and reached up and drew him down upon her. Just the taut length of his body covering hers made her heart sing. The gown she wore was worked up and off her. The white cotton fell into a heap beside the bed, along with his pajama bottoms. As Killian settled back against her, he grazed her flushed cheek.

"You're so brave. So brave..." And she was, in a way Killian had never seen in a woman before. Knowing gave him the courage to reach out and love her as he'd torridly dreamed of doing so many times. As he slid his fingers up across her rib cage to caress her breast, he felt her tense in anticipation. This time, Susannah deserved all he could give her. There was no hurry now, no threat of danger. His mouth pulled into a taut line, somewhere between a smile of pleasure and a grimace of agony, as she pressed her hips against him.

The silent language she shared with him brought tears to his eyes. Susannah wasn't passive. No, she responded, initiated, and matched his hunger for her. When her hands drifted down across his waist and caressed him, he trembled violently. His world, always held in tight control, began to melt as her lips molded against his and her hands ignited him. He surrendered to the strength of this woman who loved him with a blinding fierceness that he was only beginning to understand.

As he slid his hand beneath her hips, Susannah closed her eyes, her fingers resting tensely against his damp, bunched shoulders. Her world was heat, throbbing heat, and filled with such aching longing that she gave a small whimper of pleading when he hesitated fractionally. The ache intensified. Without thinking, guided only by her desire to give and receive, Susannah moved with a primal timelessness that enveloped them. They were like living, breathing embers, smoldering, then blazing to bright, hungry life within each other's arms.

As Killian surged powerfully into her, he gripped her, as if she represented his one tenuous hold on life. In those spinning, molten moments when they gave the gift of themselves to one another, he felt real hope for the first time since he had lost his family. Glorying in his burgeoning love for Susannah, Killian sank against her, breathing raggedly.

Gently he tamed several strands of her sable hair away from her dampened brow. His smile was vulnerable as she opened her eyes and gazed dazedly up into his face. What right did he have to tell Susannah he loved her? Did he dare hope that she could stand the brutal terrors that plagued him night after night? Was he asking too much of her, even though she was willing to try?

Tasting again her wet, full mouth, Killian trembled. He didn't have those answers—as badly as he wanted them. There was so much to say to Susannah, to share with her. He lost himself in her returning ardor, for now unwilling to look beyond the moment.

With a groan, Killian came to her side and brought her into his arms. "You're sunlight," he rasped, sliding his fingers through her tangled hair. "Hope and sunlight, all woven together like some kind of mystical tapestry."

The words feathered through Susannah. Sean held her so tightly—as if he were afraid that, like the sun, she would disappear, to be replaced by the awful darkness that stalked him. With a trembling smile, she closed her eyes and pressed the length of herself against him. He'd used the word *hope*. That was enough of a step for now, she thought hazily. The word *love* had never crossed his lips. But she had to be patient and wait for Sean to reveal his love for her, if that was what it was after all. Susannah didn't try to fool herself by thinking that, just because they shared the beauty of loving each other physically, it meant that Sean came to her with real love. She would have to wait and hope that he loved her in return. Whispering his name, she said, "I'm so tired...."

"Sleep, colleen. Sleep," he coaxed thickly. As much as he wanted to love her again, to silently show her his love for her, Killian knew sleep was best. He might be a selfish bastard, but he wasn't that selfish. Refusing to take advantage of the situation, he absorbed her wonderful nearness, wanting nothing more out of life than this exquisite moment.

Lying awake for a good hour after Susannah had quickly dropped off to sleep, Killian stared up at the plaster ceiling. How could she have known that he needed this? Needed her in his arms? Her soft, halting words, laced with tears, haunted him. Susannah loved him—without reserve. Didn't she know what she was getting into? He was a hopeless mess of black emotions that ruled his nights and stalked his heels during the day.

His mouth tightening, Killian absently stroked her silky hair, thinking how each strand, by itself, was weak. Yet a thick group of strands was strong. Maybe that was symbolic of Susannah. She was strong right now, while he'd never felt weaker or more out of control.

Sighing, Killian moved his head and pressed a chaste kiss to her fragrant hair. He'd cried tonight, for the first time in his life. Oddly, he felt cleaner, lighter. His stomach still ached from the wrenching sobs that had torn from him, and he absently rubbed his abdomen. The tears had taken the weight of years of grief away from him. And Susannah had paid a price to reach inside him to help him.

Closing his eyes, his arms around Susannah, Killian slid into a dreamless sleep—a sleep that was profoundly deep and healing. His first such sleep since the day he'd become a soldier in the French Foreign Legion.

Killian awoke with a start. *Susannah?* Instantly, he lifted his head and twisted it to the right. She was gone! Sunlight poured in through the ivory sheers—a blinding, joyous radiance flooding the room and making him squint. Quickly he sat up. The clock on the dresser read 11:00. *Impossible!* Killian muttered an exclamation to himself as he threw his legs across the bed and stood up. How could it be this late?

Fear twisted his heart. *Susannah.* Where was she? Had she left him after awaking this morning? Had she realized just how much of a liability he would be in her life? Bitterness coated his mouth as he quickly opened the door and strode across the hall to his bedroom. He wouldn't blame her. What woman in her right mind would stay around someone like him?

Killian hurried through a quick, hot shower and changed into a pair of tan chino slacks and a dark blue polo shirt. He padded quickly down the hall and realized that not only were the heavily draped windows in the living room open, they were raised. A slight breeze, sweet and fragrant, filled the house.

"Susannah?" His voice was off-key. Killian quickly looked around the living room and found it empty. He heard no sound from the kitchen, but hurried there anyway. Each beat of his heart said, *Susannah is gone.* A fist of emotion pushed its way up through his chest, and tears stung his eyes. Tears! Killian didn't care as he bounded into the kitchen.

Everything looked in order. Nothing out of place— and no Susannah. Killian stood there, his hand pressed against his eyes, and gripped the counter for support. She was gone. The shattering discovery overwhelmed him, and all he could do was feel the hot sting of tears entering his closed eyes as he tasted her loss.

The laughter of women vaguely registered on his spinning senses. Killian snapped his head toward the window. Outside, down by the lawn leading to the oceanfront, Susannah stood with his gardener, Mrs. Johnston.

His fingers whitened against the counter, and it took precious seconds for him to find his balance. Susannah hadn't left! She'd stayed! Killian stood rooted to the spot, his eyes narrowing on the two women. Susannah wore a simple white blouse, jeans, and sensible brown shoes. Her glorious hair was plaited into one long braid that hung between her shoulder blades. She stood talking animatedly with the gray-haired older woman.

Relief, sharp and serrating, jagged down through Killian. Susannah was still here. He hung his head, feeling a mass of confused emotions boiling up within him. He loved Susannah. He loved her. As he raised his head, he felt many things becoming clear. Things he had to talk to Susannah about. What would her reaction be? He had to tell her the truth, and she had to listen. What then? Killian wasn't at all sure how Susannah would judge him and his sordid world. What he did know was what he wanted: to wake up with this woman every morning for the rest of his life. But could he ask that of her?

Susannah waved goodbye to Mrs. Johnston as she left. Turning, she went through the front door of the beautifully kept cottage. In the living room she came to a startled halt.

"Sean."

He stood near the couch. The surprise on her features turned to concern. Killian searched her face ruthlessly for any telltale sign that she had changed her mind about him since last night. He opened his hand.

"When I got up, you were gone. I thought you'd left."

Susannah saw the suffering in his dark eyes. "Left?" She moved toward where he stood uncertainly.

"Yeah, forever." Killian grimaced. "Not that I'd blame you if you did."

Susannah smiled softly as she halted in front of him. Killian was stripped of his worldly defenses, standing nakedly vulnerable before her. Sensing his fragile state, she gently reached out and touched his stubbled cheek.

"I'm in for the long haul," she said, holding his haunted gaze. "If you'll let me be, Sean."

A ragged sigh tore from him, and he gripped her hand in his. "Then we need to sit down and do some serious talking, Susannah."

"Okay." She followed him to the couch. When he sat down facing her, she tucked her legs beneath her. Her knees were touching his thigh. His face was ravaged-looking, and his eyes were still puffy from sleep.

"Last night," Killian began thickly, reaching out and grazing her skin, "I could have hurt you." He felt shaky inside, on the verge of crying again as he rested his hand on her shoulder. "After my parents were murdered, Meg and I were given to foster parents to raise. I guess we were lucky, because we had no family left back in Ireland, so Immigration decided to let us stay. Our foster parents were good to us. Meg really blossomed under their love and care."

"And you?"

Sean shrugged. "I was angry and moody most of the time. I wanted to kill the two boys who had murdered our parents. I didn't do well at school. In fact,

I skipped it most of the time and got mixed up in gang activities. Meg, on the other hand, was doing very well. She began acting in drama classes at high school, and she was good. Really good.''

Susannah saw the pain in Sean's features. No longer did he try to hide behind that implacable, emotionless mask. His eyes were raw with uncertainty and his turbulent emotions. Reaching out, she covered his hand with hers. ''How did you get into the Foreign Legion?''

''I joined the French Foreign Legion when I was seventeen, after running away from home. I had a lot of anger, Susannah, and no place to let it go. I was always in fights with other gang members. I saw what I was doing to my foster parents, to Meg, and I decided to get out of their lives.

''The Legion was hard, Susannah. Brutal and hard. It kills men who don't toughen up and walk a straight line of harsh discipline. By the time they found out my real age, I'd been in a year and survived, so they didn't kick me out. Most of my anger had been beaten out of me by that time, or released in the wartime situations we were called in to handle.

''I was only in a year when my company was sent to Africa to quell a disturbance.'' Killian withdrew his hand and stared down at the couch, the poisonous memories boiling up in him. ''I won't tell you the gory details, but it was bloody. Tribesmen were fighting one another, and we had to try and intercede and keep the peace. For three years I was in the middle of a bloodbath that never stopped. I saw such inhumanity. I thought I knew what violence was, because I'd grown up in Northern Ireland, where it's a way of life, but this was a hundred times worse.''

"And a hundred times more haunting?"

Her soft voice cut through the terror, through the revulsion that dogged him. When she slid her hand into his, he gripped it hard. "Yeah—the basis for most of my nightmares.

"The Legion has no heart, no feelings, Susannah. No one in the company slept well at night—everyone had nightmares. To combat it, to try to find an escape, I took up karate." He released her and held up his hand, his voice bleak. "All I did was learn how to kill another way. I was a natural, and when my captain realized it, he promoted me and made me an instructor to the legionnaires stationed with me. Just doing the hard physical work took the edge off my time in Africa.

"And then, *Sous-Lieutenant* Morgan Trayhern was transferred into my company as an assistant company commander. He had a lot of problems, too, and we just kind of gravitated toward each other over a period of a year. We both found some solace in each other's friendship. Morgan kept talking about creating a private company of mercenaries like ourselves. He wanted to pursue the idea once his hitch was up with the Legion.

"I liked the idea. I hated the Legion, the harsh discipline. Some of the men needed that kind of brutality, but I didn't. I was getting out after my six-year obligation was up, so I began to plan my life for the future. I told Morgan I'd join his company if he ever wanted to try it." Gently he recaptured Susannah's hand, grateful for her silence. She was absorbing every word he said.

"Then we had trouble in Africa again, and my company parachuted into a hot landing zone. It was the same thing all over again—only the tribes' names had changed. But this time both tribes turned on us and tried to wipe us out."

Susannah gasped, and her fingers closed tightly over Killian's scarred hand.

His mouth twisted. "Morgan was facing a situation similar to the one he had in Vietnam. We lost eighty percent of our company, Susannah. It was a living hell. I thought we were all going to die, but Morgan pulled us out. I saved his life during that time. Finally, at the last moment, he got the air support he'd requested. We were all wounded. It was just a question of how badly. Before both tribes hit us with a final assault, we were lifted out by helicopter." His voice grew bitter. "All the rest, every last valiant man who had died, were left behind."

"How awful . . ."

Killian sighed raggedly. "Last night I lay awake a long time with you in my arms, reviewing my life." He gently turned her hand over in his, realizing how soft and feminine she was against him. "I was born into violence, colleen. I've done nothing but lead a violent life. Last year, Morgan sent three of us down to work with the Peruvian police to clean up a cocaine connection. Wolf, a member of our team, got captured by the local drug lord. I went in to save him, and I ended up getting captured, too."

Susannah's eyes widened. "What happened?"

"The drug lord was real good at what he did to us," was all he would say. He still wanted to protect Susannah, somehow, from the ugliness of his world. "He had us for a month before Jake, the third member of our team, busted in and brought down the drug lord. Wolf was nearly dead, and I wasn't too far behind him. We got flown stateside by the CIA, and we both recuperated in a naval hospital near the capital. As soon as Wolf regained consciousness, he told Morgan he wanted out, that he couldn't handle being a mercenary any longer."

With a little laugh, Killian said, "At the time, I remember thinking Wolf had lost the edge it takes to stay alive in our business. He's part Indian, so he stayed pretty much to himself. So did I. But I admired his guts when he told Morgan 'no more.' Morgan didn't call him a coward. Instead, he saw to it that Wolf got a job as a forest ranger up in Montana."

With a shake of his head, Killian whispered, "I envied Wolf for having the courage to quit. I wanted to, but I thought everyone would see me as a coward."

Hope leaped into Susannah's eyes, and it was mirrored in her voice. "You want to quit?"

"I can't," Killian said quietly, searching her glowing features, clinging to the hope in her eyes. "Part of my check goes to pay for my sister's massive medical bills. But..."

"What?"

He gripped his hands, thinking how small, yet how strong, she was. "I'm messed up inside, Susannah. Maybe I've done this work too long and don't know any other way." His voice grew thick. "Last night, when I held you, I realized that I needed to get help— professional help—to unravel this nightmare that's eating me alive from the inside out. I swore I'd never put you in that kind of jeopardy again."

With a little cry, Susannah threw her arms around Killian's shoulders. "I love you so much," she whispered, tears squeezing from her eyes. She felt his arms slide around her and bring her tightly against him.

Killian buried his face in her hair. "It can be done, Sean. I know it can."

He shook his head, and when he spoke again his voice was muffled. "I don't know that, Susannah."

She eased away just enough to study his suffering features. "I'll be here for you, if you want...."

The words, sweet and filled with hope, fell across his tightly strung nerves. He searched her lustrous eyes. "I don't know...." How badly he wanted to confess his love to her, and yet he couldn't. "Let me feel my way through this."

"Do you want me to leave?" She hated to ask the question. But she did ask it, and then she held her breath.

"I— No, not really." He held her hand tightly within his. "That's the selfish side of me speaking. The other side, the nightmares... Well, you'd be better off staying at a nearby hotel—just in case."

Susannah had faith that Killian would never harm her, no matter how virulent his nightmares became, but she knew it wasn't her place to make that decision. "I have the next three weeks off, Sean. My principal gave me the time because he felt after all the trauma I'd gone through I needed time to pull myself together again."

Killian's heart thudded, and he lifted his head. "Three weeks?" Three weeks of heaven. There was such love shining in her eyes that he clung to the tenuous shred of hope that had begun burning in his chest when he loved Susannah last night.

"Yes...."

He compressed his lips and studied her long, slender fingers. The nails were cut short because she did so much gardening, Killian realized. Susannah had hands of the earth, hands that were in touch with the primal elements of nature—and her touch brought out so much in him that was good. "I'll take you to a hotel in downtown Victoria," he told her quietly. "I want you to stay these three weeks if you want, Susannah." He lifted his gaze and met hers. "No promises."

She shook her head, her mouth growing dry. "No...no promises. A day at a time, Sean."

Susannah gave him a trembling smile and framed his lean, harsh face between her soft hands. "You slept the whole night last night without those dreams coming back?"

Killian nodded. "It was the first night I've slept that hard. Without waking up." He knew there was awe in his voice at the revelation.

Susannah gave him a tender smile. "Because you trusted yourself on some level. The situation was important enough for you to reach out and try to change it."

There was food for thought in her assessment. A little more of the tension within him dissolved. "I want to live now, in the present," he told her, capturing her hands. "I want to take you sailing this morning, if you'd like." He gestured toward the wooden dock at the edge of the water. "I've got a forty-foot yacht that I've worked on for the past eight years, between assignments. I've always been good with wood, so I began to build the boat as something to do when I got back here."

"Because you couldn't sleep?" Susannah's heart broke for him.

"Partly." He managed to quirk a smile. "Then I put in the rose garden around the house. I find keeping busy keeps me from remembering."

"Then let's go sailing. I've never done it before, but I'm willing to try."

Sunlight glanced off the dark blue of the ocean as the yacht, the *Rainbow*, slipped cleanly through the slight swells of early afternoon. Susannah sat with Killian at the stern of the yacht. He stood proudly at the helm, his focus on the sails as the wind filled them, taking them farther away from the coast of the island. The first time the yacht had heeled over on her side, Susannah had let out a yelp of fear and surprise, thinking the boat would flip over and drown them. But Killian had held her and explained that the yacht would never tip over. Over the past two hours, Susannah had relaxed and enjoyed his company, the brilliant sunlight and the fresh salt breeze that played across the Strait of Juan de Fuca, where they were sailing.

"Here, hold the wheel," he said. Killian saw the surprise in her wide eyes. He smiled and held out his hand. Just being on the water helped to clear his mind and emotions.

"But—"

"I need to change the sails," he explained, reaching down and gripping her fingers. "Don't you want to learn about sailing?" he said teasingly as he drew her to her feet and placed her beside him at the wheel.

"Sure, but—"

Killian stood directly behind her, his body providing support and shelter for her as he placed her hands on the wheel. His mouth near her ear, he said, "I'm going to shift the sails from port to starboard. Be sure and duck when the boom comes across the cockpit.

Otherwise, you'll be knocked overboard, and I don't want that to happen.''

"Are you sure I can do this?" Susannah was wildly aware of Killian's body molded against hers. The feeling was making her want him all over again. As she twisted a look up at him, she felt her heart expand with a discovery that nearly overwhelmed her. His hair was ruffled by the breeze, and there was real joy in his deep blue eyes. For the first time, she was seeing Sean happy.

"Very sure." He leaned down and pressed his lips to her temple. The strands of her hair were silky beneath his exploration. Susannah invited spontaneity, and Killian reveled in the quick, hot kiss she gave him in answer.

"All right, I'll try," she said, her heart beating hard from his closeness.

"Just remember to duck," he warned, and left her in charge of guiding the yacht.

At two o'clock, they dropped anchor in a small crescent-shaped bay. Thrilled with the way the day was revealing itself, Susannah helped Sean tuck the sails away before the anchor was dropped. He motored the vessel into the dark blue bay, which was surrounded by tall evergreens on three sides. A great blue heron with a seven-foot wing span had been hunting frogs or small fish in the shallows, and it took off just as their anchor splashed into the water.

Susannah watched in awe as the magnificent bird swept by, just above the mast, and headed around the tip of the island. She turned just in time to see that Killian was watching the huge crane, too.

"She was breathtaking," Susannah confided as she moved toward the galley. Killian had promised her lunch, and she was hungry.

Sean nodded. "What I'm looking at is breathtaking," he murmured, and he reached out and captured her. The yacht was very stable at anchor; the surface of the bay smooth and unruffled. Susannah came willingly into his arms, closed her eyes and rested against his tall, lean form. His voice had been low and vibrating, sending a wonderful sheet of longing through her.

Killian absorbed Susannah against him, her natural scent, the fragrance of her shining sable hair, intoxicating him. "I feel like a thief," he murmured near her ear, savoring the feel of her arms tightening around him. "I feel like I'm stealing from you before I get thrown back into the way things were before you stepped into my life."

Gently disengaging from him, just enough that she could meet and hold his gaze, Susannah nodded. Her love for him was so fierce, so steadfast, that she wasn't threatened by his admission. "I remember a number of times in my folks' marriage when they went through stormy times," she confided. "They love each other, Sean, and Ma often told me when I'd grown up and we talked about those stormy periods that love held them together. I like the way Ma sees love, Sean. She calls it a fabric that she and Pa wove together. Some threads were very strong. Others were weak and sometimes frayed or even broke. She saw those weak times as fix-it times. It didn't mean they weren't afraid. But the one thing they clung to throughout those times was the fact that they loved each other."

He rested his jaw against her hair, absorbing her story. "I've never thought of love as a fabric."

"Look at your parents," Susannah said. "Were they happy together?"

He nodded and closed his eyes, savoring her nearness and allowing her husky voice to touch his heart. "Very happy."

"And did they fight from time to time?"

"Often," he chuckled, suddenly recalling those times. "My mother was a red-haired spitfire. My father was dark-haired and closed up tighter than the proverbial drum. When she suggested we emigrate to America, my father balked at the idea. My mother was the explorer, the person who would take risks."

"And your father was content to remain conservative and have the status quo."

Killian nodded and grazed her flushed cheek. Susannah's sparkling gray eyes made him aware of just how much she loved him. "Yes. But in the end, my mother pioneered getting us to America. It took many years to make her dream for all of us come true, but she did it."

Susannah asked soberly, "Do you blame your mother for what happened a year after you emigrated?"

Killian shook his head. "No. I wanted to move as much as she did."

"You're more like your mother?"

"Very much."

"A risk-taker."

"I guess I am."

Susannah held his thoughtful gaze. She could feel Sean thinking, weighing and measuring things they'd spoken about from the past and placing them like a transparency on the present—perhaps on their situation. Did he love her? He'd never said so, but in her heart, she felt he must—or as close as he could come to loving someone in his present state.

"I like," she said softly, "thinking about a relationship in terms of a tapestry. Ma always said she and Pa wove a very colorful one, filled with some tragedy, but many happy moments, too."

Gently Killian moved his hands down her slender arms, and then back up to rest on her shoulders. "A tapestry is a picture, too."

"Yes, it is."

"How do you see the tapestry of your life?" he asked quietly.

She shrugged and gave a slight smile, enjoying his rough, callused hands caressing her. "I see teaching handicapped children as important to my life. I certainly didn't see getting shot and being in a coma or having a contract put out on me, but that's a part of my tapestry now." She frowned. "I guess, having that unexpected experience, I understand how precious life is. Before, Sean, I took life for granted. I saw myself being a teacher, someday meeting a man who would love me, and then marrying. I want children, but not right away. I saw my folks' wisdom in not having children right away. It gave them a chance to solidify and work on their marriage. By the time Denny came along, they were emotionally ready for him. By the time I came along, they were more than ready." She smiled fondly. "I had a very happy childhood compared to most children. But I feel part of it was my parents' being older and more mature, more settled and sure of who they were."

"A tapestry that had the scales of life woven into it," he mused, holding her softened gaze.

"I never thought of it in symbolic terms, but yes, a balancing between doing something I love and having a husband and children when we're both ready for them, for the responsibility of raising them the best we can."

"You've brought balance into my life," Killian admitted, watching her eyes flare, first with surprise, then with joy. "I fought against it."

"Because you were scared."

"I still am," he told her wryly, and eased away.

Susannah followed him into the tight little galley below. There was a small table with a wraparound sofa, and she sat down to watch him fix their lunch at the kitchen area.

"I was scared to come and see you," she admitted.

Twisting a look over his shoulder as he prepared roast beef sandwiches, he said, "I couldn't believe you were standing there, Susannah."

"Your head or your heart?"

Her question was as insightful as she was about him. His mouth curved faintly as he forced himself to finish putting the sandwiches together. Placing the plate of them on the table, he brought over a bag of potato chips. "My head."

Susannah watched as he brought two bottles of mineral water from the small refrigerator built into the teakwood bulkhead. His entire face was relaxed, with none of the tension that was normally there. Even his mouth, usually a hard line holding back some emotional barrage, was softer.

"And your heart?" she asked in a whisper as he sat down next to her.

"My heart," he sighed, "in some way expected to see you." As he passed the sandwich to her, he met and caught her gaze. "I'm finding out that talking about how I feel isn't so bad after all."

With a little laugh, Susannah said, "Silence is the bane of all men. This society has bludgeoned you with the idea that you shouldn't feel, shouldn't cry and shouldn't speak of your emotions. It's a learned thing, Sean, and it's something you can change. That's the good news."

As he bit into his sandwich, Killian felt another cloak of dread dissolve around his shoulders. "You make it easy to talk," he admitted. "It's you. Something about you."

Melting beneath his intense, heated gaze, Susannah forced herself to eat the sandwich she didn't taste. Would Sean make good on his decision to send her away tonight? Or would he have the courage to let her remain? Her heart whispered that if he would allow her to stay with him tonight, his trust in himself and in her was strong enough that he could come to grips with his nightmare-ridden nights very quickly.

Nothing was ever changed in one day, Susannah reminded herself. But life demanded some awfully big steps if one genuinely wanted to heal. If Sean could trust in her love for him, never mind the fact that he might not return her love in the same measure, he could use her support in healing his past.

Only tonight would tell, Susannah ruminated. Being a victim of violence had taught her about the moment, the hour, the day. She would take each moment with Sean as a gift, instead of leaping ahead to wonder what his decision might be.

* * *

Just as they entered Sean's home, his phone rang. Susannah saw him frown as he hurried to the wall phone in the kitchen to answer it.

"Hello? Meg?" Killian shot a glance over at Susannah, who stood poised at the entrance to the living room. Surprised that his sister had called, he saw Susannah smile and disappear. She didn't have to leave, but it was too late to call her back. Wrestling with his shock over his sister's call, Killian devoted all his attention to her.

Susannah wisely left the kitchen. Going to her bedroom, she slowly began to pack her one and only bag to leave for the hotel in Victoria. She'd seen shock and puzzlement register on Sean's face over Meg's call. Didn't they talk often? Her heart wasn't in packing her clothes. The bed where they had lain, where they had made love, still contained the tangle of covers. Susannah ached to stay the night, to show Sean that two people could help his problem, not make it worse.

Killian was just coming out of the kitchen after the call when he saw Susannah placing her suitcase by the door. He shoved his hands into his pockets and moved toward her.

Straightening, Susannah felt her heartbeat pick up as Killian approached her. He wore a quizzical expression on his face, and she sensed that something important had occurred. She curbed her questions. Sean had to trust her enough to share, and not make her pull everything out of him.

"The funniest thing just happened," he murmured as he came to a halt in front of her. "Meg just called. I can't believe it." He shook his head.

"Believe what?"

"Meg just told me that she contacted Ian. She's asked him to fly to Ireland to see her." He gave Susannah a long, intense look.

"Wonderful!" Susannah clapped her hands together. "That's wonderful!"

"Yes . . . it is. . . ."

"What led her to that decision?" she asked breathlessly, seeing the hope burning in Killian's dark eyes.

"She said he'd somehow found out where she was living and sent her a long letter. He talked about his love being strong enough to support both of them through this time in her life. All along, Meg loved Ian, but she was afraid he'd leave her as soon as he saw her disfigurement." Again Killian shook his head. "I'll be damned. The impossible has happened. I'm really glad for her. For Ian. They're both good people, caught in a situation they didn't make for themselves."

Reaching out, Susannah gently touched his arm. "The same could be said of you. Of us, Sean."

He stood very still, hearing the pain, the hope, in Susannah's voice, and seeing it reflected in her eyes.

Risking everything, she whispered, "Sean, you could send me away, just as Meg sent Ian away. Only you would be sending me away just for the night hours that you fear so much. She sent him away for several years, because of her fear that she would be rejected. In a way," she said, in a low, unsteady voice, "you're doing the same thing to me. You're afraid if I stay, you'll hurt me."

Her fingers tightening around his arm, Susannah stepped closer. "I know it isn't true, but you don't. At least not yet. But if you're searching for proof, Sean, look at last night. You didn't have nightmares haunt you after we slept in each other's arms, did you?''

"No...I didn't...." He stood there, assimilating the urgency in her heartfelt words. Realization shattered him in those moments. Meg had finally realized that Ian's love for her was steady—that it wasn't going to be pulled away from her, no matter how bad the situation appeared. He studied Susannah intently. He wasn't really questioning her love for him; he was questioning his ability to love her despite his wounding. Just as Meg had done, in a slightly different way.

Running his fingers through his hair, he muttered, "Stay tonight, Susannah. Please?"

Her heart leaped with joy, but she remained very quiet beneath his inspection. "Yes, I'd like that, darling, more than anything..."

With a groan, Killian swept her into his arms. He buried his face in her hair. "I love you, Susannah. I've loved you from the beginning, and I was too stupid, too scared, to admit it to myself, to you...."

The words, harsh with feeling, flowed across Susannah. Murmuring his name over and over again, she sought and found his mouth. The courage to admit his love for her was, perhaps, the biggest step of all. Drowning in the heated splendor of his mouth, being held so tightly that the breath was squeezed from her, Susannah returned his fire. Tears leaked from beneath her closed eyes, dampening her lashes and then her cheeks.

As Killian eased from her lips, he took his thumbs and removed those tears of happiness. His own eyes were damp, and the relief he felt was sharp and deep.

"I want to try," he rasped as he framed her upturned face. "It isn't going to be easy."

"No," she quavered, "it won't be. But our tapestry will be strong, because of our courage to grow—together, darling."

"I'm afraid of tonight, colleen."

"We'll be afraid together. We'll hold each other. We'll talk. We'll do whatever it takes, Sean."

She was right. "One day at a time. One night at a time." Never had Killian wanted anything to work as much as he did this. He'd never admitted loving another woman. He'd been too fearful to do that. Susannah's strength, her undiluted belief in him, was giving him the courage to try.

"There will be good nights and bad ones, I'm sure," Susannah warned. "We can't expect miracles."

He smiled a little. "You're the miracle in my life. I'll do whatever I have to in order to keep you."

His commitment was more than she'd ever dreamed of hearing from him. Somehow Meg's courage to release her past had helped him see his own situation differently. "Just trying is enough," Susannah told him simply. And it was.

Epilogue

Susannah's heart wasn't in her packing. Her three weeks on Vancouver Island had fled by like a blink of the eye. Killian was quieter than usual as he helped her take her clothes out of the closet.

He was thinking about something important, and she could feel it. The days had been wonderful days of discovery, of joy and exploration. The nights had been a roller-coaster ride of good and bad. Together they had managed to confront Killian's nightmare past, and with some success.

More than anything, Killian knew he needed professional help to completely change for good. They'd talked about it and agreed that Susannah couldn't be the linchpin of his healing. He saw her as a loving support, his primary cheerleader. But it wasn't her responsibility to heal him. It was his.

The suitcase was packed, and she snapped it shut. As she turned around, Killian brought her into his arms.

"I've got a few phone calls to make before I take you to the airport."

"Okay." One day at a time, she reminded herself. Sean had not spoken of anything beyond her three weeks at his house. As badly as Susannah wanted to know his future plans and how they included her, she didn't ask.

"I want you to be there when I make the call."

She searched his shadowed face. "Who are you going to talk to?"

"Morgan."

Her heart thudded once. "Morgan?"

"Yes."

"Why?"

Killian cupped her face and looked deep into her wide, loving eyes. "To tell him I'm asking for permanent reassignment to the U.S. only. I'm also telling him I want jobs that don't involve violence. He's got some of those available. Mercenaries are more than just men of war. Sometimes a mercenary is needed just to be eyes and ears. I'm going to tell him I want low-risk short-term assignments." He smiled uncertainly. "That way, I can make my home in Glen, Kentucky, and keep putting my life back together with you."

Tears jammed into her eyes. "Oh, Sean..." She threw her arms around his shoulders.

"It's not going to be easy," he warned her grimly, taking her full weight.

"We'll do it together," Susannah said, her voice muffled against his chest.

Killian knew it could be the worst kind of hell at times, but Susannah's unwavering support, her love for him, had made the decision easy. He held her tightly. "Together," he rasped thickly. "Forever."

* * * * *

Silhouette
SPECIAL EDITION®

MORGAN'S MERCENARIES

by
Lindsay McKenna

Morgan Trayhern has returned and he's set up a company full of best pals in adventure. Three men who've been to hell and back are about to fight the toughest battle of all...love!

You loved Wolf Harding in HEART OF THE WOLF (SE #818), so be sure to catch the other two stories in this exciting trilogy. Sean Killian a.k.a. THE ROGUE (SE #824) is coming your way in July. And in August it's COMMANDO (SE #830) with hero Jake Randolph.

These are men you'll love and stories you'll treasure...only from Silhouette Special Edition!

MEN · MADE IN AMERICA

Fifty red-blooded, white-hot, true-blue hunks from every State in the Union!

Beginning in May, look for MEN MADE IN AMERICA! Written by some of our most popular authors, these stories feature fifty of the strongest, sexiest men, each from a different state in the union!

Two titles available every other month at your favorite retail outlet.

In July, look for:

CALL IT DESTINY by Jayne Ann Krentz (Arizona)
ANOTHER KIND OF LOVE by Mary Lynn Baxter (Arkansas)

In September, look for:

DECEPTIONS by Annette Broadrick (California)
STORMWALKER by Dallas Schulze (Colorado)

You won't be able to resist MEN MADE IN AMERICA!